# The Submissive Widow

*Calvin Himel*

# The Submissive Widow

First Printing:
## ISBN:
## EPUB-ISBN:
Cover Art by: Lemih

# Other Stories from the Author

Location of Love
2019
Supermarket Love Affair &
    Three Short Stories
1.Special Love
2. Alien Love Affair
3. Cheating Wife     2019
Four Girls plus One
2019
The Submissive Widow
2020
The Story of Master Caesar
2020
The Family
2020

# Introduction

I would like to thank again my wife who if it wasn't for her insistence, that I find something to do, this body of work and all of my other stories wouldn't exist, and her help as my avid proof reader.

I would like to dedicate this book to all the wonderful people who have been a part of my life, both in the past and present, and to those who I may have had just a brief encounter, meaning full or not. And to those both living and dead who have made our small planet such a wonderful place to live. I know some may disagree with that statement, as I hope and pray that love, peace and a life of joy finds you, or you find it in your daily quest.

Sincerely: Calvin Louis Himel
February, 08, 2020

# The Submissive Widow

# One

Every day we live is new and challenging, and since the only constant in life is change, we must be prepared for challenges, opportunities, and even calamities that will come our way. Some come directly, and others indirectly, whether we are looking for them or not. Sometimes things and people are placed in our lives and time must pass before we find out why. Another thing is you have to be careful of is what you think about sometimes, and particularly what you might wish for, as thoughts have a way of manifesting themselves without you being aware of their close presence. They could be all around you, and maybe you may not even recognize them until it's too late. Few people recognize or realize it, but the power of the spoken word is also another very powerful tool also that affects our daily lives.

This is the story about what happened one day in that particular moment of time to Carl Hogan, an ordinary guy, a good and very loving, caring and most charming individual by modern standards, who always strived to make a success of his life and had a taste for the unusual sometimes as many of us probably do. He worked his ordinary job as an air conditioning and heating technician and continued to strive and make progress in his life and soon obtained and became a licensed plumber and electrician and eventually ended up owning his own business and employing several others in his very own small startup company. As time went on his business prospered and the number of people he employed slowly but gradually began to increase in proportion to his growing business opportunities. He eventually began selling the equipment he repaired and serviced and soon began enjoying his job even more and the comradery with his small group of loyal employees as his small but highly successful company slowly began to grow over the years. Business was always very good and very consistent as he always had jobs lined up and was usually booked several weeks in advance for major installations even from the beginning of starting out and operating on his very own and always having several contracts most of the time for complete whole house heating and air conditioning system installations especially in newly constructed homes which became very profitable for Carl when the economy expanded and permitted new home construction to flourish. He always had customers for his needed regular maintenance services, and this was one of the reasons for his continuing growth and steady income even when the economy wasn't doing particularly well. Several of his employees held dual licensees in the building trades just like himself, and that allowed him to pursue even larger jobs without any hesitation, as his small business thrived and continued to grow at a very reasonable and steady pace.

Carl Hogan was now thirty five, single, very handsome and came from a mixed race family, his father was of German, Spanish and African American decent and his mother was Irish, Italian, African and Native American. Carl was, besides being very handsome, was six foot two, one hundred eighty pounds with a smooth light olive completion which gave him an exotic appearance with his large curly auburn hair and would often make people wonder about his ethnic origins or what his nationality really was a many times. He would always check the box for other; when filling out job applications before he ever had any idea of starting his very own company, ever since when he first started working while attending high school. And once he became an employer, he made it a point of employing the most qualified people in the field and especially any qualified minorities he could find, even women. He had some of the most competent employees in the business. The quality of their work had helped him earn a very good reputation and they were known far and wide for doing outstanding quality work, and were considered some of the most competent and qualified technicians in their field. Carl had built his business on exceptional work quality, timely response, and complete satisfaction along with fair pricing, and also had built over time an exceptionally good overall reputation in the business. Carl eventually had to purchase three of the new hi cube work vans after the first one he started out with, which he purchased second hand and another, the second vehicle he had bought used also soon after he had hired his first full time crew, just quit working around the same time as well after many miles and years of serious wear and tear. Carl's crews were paired up most of the time so the work would be completed in a more timely fashion, it worked out very well with only one man operating alone for emergency calls most of the time. He paid his employees very well; they were all union members just like Carl. His employees were loyal to him and would go out of

8

their way to help him maintain the small company's excellent reputation for on time service.

Carl being a single man, and divorced didn't have a regular girlfriend or anyone special after having been married just once after coming out of the army at the age of twenty two after spending three years where he reached the rank of specialist, or E4. He met and married a young woman he though he loved but really just wanted some regular sex and didn't think much at the time about being married. She already had a child, a young girl who was four years old at the time. Carl was married to her for almost five years until she returned from work very late one evening as he and the step daughter were sitting together and looking at television. She entered the living room where they were living and asked him to move out, and told her daughter to move upstairs with her grandmother. At the time they stayed in a garden apartment in her mother's house and Carl just said, give me a month and just moved out without any hesitation before the end of the month since he didn't have anything but his clothes and a few books and his tools. She worked in a night club and was having on and off again affairs with other men and Carl suspected something was going on, but at the time he wasn't a saint either and had several affairs around the same time himself. It wasn't a good or wholesome marriage to begin with anyway. He just had a feeling something was about to happen and really wasn't surprised when his wife asked him to move on and out. He soon after filed for a divorce since he had already placed a disclaimer add in the local newspaper two days before, which at the time back then wasn't a problem since he owned nothing but his car, and his wife had bought her own anyway also. Carl moved out and into a studio apartment in a high rise on the other side of the city before finishing the trade school course which he only had a couple months to go before finishing and all the while he was working full time as a bus mechanic and soon getting his apprentice ship in the electrical trades first, then the plumbing trades and finally in heating ventilation and air conditioning after the government required a new federal license because of the tightening restrictions on refrigerants which was offered on his job at the transit authority. Carl took the test, passed and qualified for the universal license, this allowed him to work on anything with refrigerant, from small appliances to industrial air conditioning systems, and being licensed in each field and using his veterans benefits helped pay for his schooling outside of work. Carl worked on the side on his days off and after work most of the time. Carl being multi-talented was soon in great demand because he could wire the jobs he did, and on some plumbing jobs also, like on some sump pump installations. After several years of hard and very diligent work on the side, and really no personal time, Carl bought his first work van and decided to strike out on his own with his now former part time employer recommending him for some of the newer construction jobs which demanded a lot of time and know how. He finally left the transit authority and took that giant leap of faith of now becoming self-employed; it did allow him a little more personal time since most jobs were done during the daylight hours. It wasn't too long after that, when Carl met and soon hired John Roberts, another recently honorably discharged army veteran like himself who was now going through the electrician apprenticeship program to help assist him. Having an assistant meant the work would be completed so much sooner and much faster now, and besides Carl had a comrade in arms and they soon developed a very close and trusting work and personal relationship. John had a family and enjoyed working for Carl and helped him build his small but growing business. As his business quickly began to pick up, Carl at first was just listed in the local telephone books, then eventually on the internet as technology continued to rapidly advance and quickly expand as the business landscape changed to being more information based. Soon after having more exposure he earned the coveted better business rating, of excellent, and soon was listed in the consumer's guide listing book for service as being highly recommended, with a very high rating for job performance that few others were able to achieve.

Carl spent all of his time, days, nights and weekends building his business and soon found a small rundown warehouse building with plenty of space inside and outside and was able to purchase it very cheaply, and then he could use it to house his few precious vehicles and would also allow him to stock the larger pieces of materials he most frequently used. He would now be able to move out of the garage he had been renting and would also allow him to now have a permanent address which would help his business grow. He spent almost all his spare time and money rebuilding the entire building and completely rehabbing it; he hired some day laborers to help him with the heavy laborious muscle work and soon turned it into a first class facility after adding a new roof, a small lunch room, locker room with showers and constructing his main office. He now had room inside an outside for several much larger vehicles and storage containers, with ample room for all his much needed electrical and plumbing supplies. He could see that it wouldn't be too much longer before he would need a much larger facility one day in a couple more years or more at the rate his business was gradually increasing and was always on the lookout for one he could purchase. He soon had to hire a combination secretary, book keeper, and telephone receptionist as his business steadily increased and the overwhelming amount of paper work that grew along with the now rapidly growing business and much sooner than he had expected. He was very fortunate when after advertising in the local newspapers for only two weeks after soon completing his new headquarters, several women applied. But out of all who applied only one person appeared to be really and truly qualified and up to the task at hand. That person was even more than qualified and much more than he could have ever hoped for. Her name was Mrs. Mary Sue Anderson, fifty two, divorced once and was now widowed. She was five foot nine, one hundred fifty pounds, very attractive and shapely, and was just the perfect person he needed to maintain his now mounting mountain of paper work, receipts, bills, invoices, payroll and taxes. Carl had built himself a very comfortable and spacious, highly efficient and well planned office on the premises for himself and one other person. And because he figured he might have to hire a secretary one day very soon had made it as comfortable as possible for a full time assistant but really hadn't expected to have to hire a secretary as soon as he did and made it as efficient and modern as possible with the latest and best office equipment available. It was where he would order the supplies he needed, keep track of his payroll and all of his other paperwork, but it was starting to become a full time job all by itself and that's the main reason he hired Mrs. Mary Sue Anderson. She was the perfect person for the job because she was an experienced executive secretary, a certified public accountant, and a notary. She had retired as a supervisor from her last job a few years earlier and could also give him some very sound business advice and was very computer savvy. During her interview, she said that she didn't want to sit around the house knitting after her last husband passed away and wanted to be in the flow of things again. She was looking forward to being involved and busy working again. After Carl decided he would hire her, which was a real no brainer, he showed her around as she complimented him on the office setup and said she would be very happy working here as he showed her what he needed done. She reassured him that there was nothing for him to worry about and within a week she had everything well under control and soon showed Carl the standard ways of keeping his account books, she also instituted streamlined accounting practices and made sure his taxes were always up to date. Carl still handled many of the smaller one man jobs himself and wasn't in the office very often and had decided to spend maybe at least three or maybe four days a week in the office and in his new warehouse area, receiving deliveries, stocking shelves, and better organizing his now growing operation. But that began to quickly change as he basically just began surveying the larger jobs he would bid on and started looking at foreclosures and doing rehabs as it started to become a major part of his operation.

He really liked being out in the field and had met many interesting people over the years and had cultivated numerous repeat customers and developed many long term business friendships which proved to be very profitable and helped him expand his business. He had also came in contact with dozens of available, single and divorced women over the years in his line of work, and many were really just outright stunning beauties and quite a few of them were really tremendous flirts. But Carl was all about the money after being married and then divorced and didn't see himself going down that path again very soon, and probably never again. He paid most women very little to no attention because he wanted so much more out of life and knew you would only achieve it through determination, and hard work and didn't mind working and putting in the extra time.

He met some women who wore next to nothing, especially when he did jobs where he was operating by himself as he sent his crews to handle the much larger and more involved jobs. He remembers vividly one time while doing a simple kitchen faucet replacement job and lying on his back under the kitchen sink. And this beautiful middle aged woman who was really talkative and also very attractive, stood right where he could see up under her dress, she had no panties on. She was extremely attractive to say the least and had recently divorced her husband after eleven years, because she said he hadn't paid any attention to her, she talked the entire time Carl was there. Carl knew she made it a point of allowing him to see her assets. He quickly finished, cleaned up and replaced all the items she had underneath the sink cabinet and handed her the bill. She paid him but must have been desperate because she then asked him if he would take her out sometimes because, she said he was really cute. Carl had to explain to her he had a company policy of no personal contact with customers and had informed his employees it wasn't a good policy to become romantically or sexually involved with any of the customers but stressed it was of course their personal choice. He didn't have to worry about that much since mostly all were happily married men, and had sometimes paired the single men up with them most of the time. Carl really did enjoy the attention women gave him but after being married, really had no real serious interest in having a steady relationship at this point in his life. He did date a few times but most of the women he found attractive and smart, were too busy with their own carriers to want or have a serious or even a steady relationship with.

When Carl was at home he enjoyed looking at pornography, with a growing collection of different films both foreign and domestic and several film shorts from around the world and really enjoyed some of the bondage videos. He looked at some internet bondage and discipline sites and the sadistic and masochistic sites he found to be really much too extreme for his personal taste, but did peak his growing curiosity. He enjoyed watching the videos with bondage, discipline and especially humiliation and would masturbate often to some of them. Carl thought he would find it hard, even difficult to actually do something like what he observed in some of the videos to another human being. He really liked and loved women very much and always thought if he did something like what he had watched in some videos, even the ones that really turned him on which were mild by bondage and discipline standards, the other person would have to really want it very much and it would have to be a part of their personality. Carl didn't think about it anymore once he relieved himself an got off, and then would continue with his normal routine around the house of cooking, washing, cleaning and relaxing.

Carl owned his own home, and along the path of building his business also became a real estate broker, that really all happened by sheer accident, mostly because of the business he was in and just for himself at first. It saved him money and sped up the process of possession after he started becoming heavily involved in rehabbing the homes he soon frequently began to purchase, because of their low selling prices. Mostly all were well constructed but needed major amounts of work. The home he was in now was the third one he lived in and only one of several he had purchased since he started his own business. He moved out of the studio apartment after he had first bought a small two story frame house, fixing it up and rehabbed it in less than eight months, then lived in it for almost a year before finding several others he soon rehabbed and then moved into as he began selling them and making a reasonable profit and just kept repeating the process. Then one day he decided to live in one which was even larger and needed even more work and living in it almost two years before selling it after finding this now current one which was about the twentieth rehab he has purchased. It was really a very comfortable home and had been a bank foreclosure for the outstanding mortgage balance but happened to be selling under the market value at the time of purchase which was kind of unusual. It wasn't very old, less than twenty years and had more space than Carl would ever really need. It didn't need any real major repairs and the ones that it did were very minor buy his standards; compared to what he usually dealt with but he always believed in keeping real estate in tip top shape, and ready to sell at any time. He had now lived here almost two years now, and was looking for something a little more upscale since his income was gradually increasing as his business slowly and steadily grew. It was more suited for a large growing family with four bedrooms of average size with the exception of the master bedroom, three full baths and two half baths with one in the large basement and another on the main floor. A fairly large living room with an open plan kitchen and dining room, not to mention a two and a half car attached garage and an ample size finished basement, and also with plenty of back yard space for children to play in. Even though he had wonderful neighbors on both sides and across the street, all were young married couples with very small to adolescent children and it was one of the reasons he knew he wouldn't be living here too much longer. When he wasn't working he would either be cleaning house or cooking, though all the rooms were empty except for his bedroom, and since the kitchen had an eat in counter with stools he didn't even have or need a kitchen table. Carl felt or rather knew this wasn't his permanent home as of yet. He thought of selling since all of his neighbors had children of various ages and it was really a family oriented neighborhood with several very good schools nearby. It almost happened when he went to a foreclosure auction on a property on half and acer, it was a very large house and when he researched it, found out it had sold for over a million dollars in the past but now the minimum opening bid now was now $600,000.00. Carl walked around the property and decided to bid on it along with several others at the same time. With his type of business and getting more into rehabbing houses all by sheer accident he could well afford taking a chance on a much higher bid at least now since all his businesses were doing well. Things were looking up and the rehabbing was paying off really well as a side business and was the main reason he ended up getting into the real estate business and having his broker's license. He attended the auction, and ended up with two smaller three bedroom homes instead which wasn't a bad outcome anyway. You have to pay cash and after having the deeds in hand proceeded to clean them out, remodel and updated the homes and shortly after, in less than six months they were back on the market again, and sold rather quickly since they were really desirable structures, and located in stable and pleasant neighborhoods and had just about doubled his money. Carl then decided and formed another company on the side, it would be located at the same business address as his primary company and had hired a small regular crew of four men who just did all his clean out and tear down work, he purchased a small dump truck and a couple more trucks they would use for hauling the tools and supplies they used. They also handled and replaced any drywall and paint after he sent in his other crews for any of the other major work, and that would include the electrical, plumbing, or air conditioning and heating.

His personal home was very sparsely decorated and other than the bed room he slept in and the kitchen, the house was empty. When Carl was home he slept most of the time, cooked and had a lawn service for his landscaping. His neighbors invited him to cook outs several times and Carl attended as often as he could. He met a few single women who also attended, but most were either, too young, too old, or too busy. He dated several on different occasions but they just weren't his type as he would find out soon after a date or two, and besides he was too busy for most women to have any kind of a really serious relationship with anyway. Carl liked being at home and that's what had prevented him from having a very serious relationship since most of the women he seemed to meet wanted to be taken out frequently, wined and dined which just wasn't his style, he liked being at home, cooking, relaxing and smoking an occasional joint .

Carl happened upon and found by chance a small trailer park that was for sale that had fallen into serious disrepair, just about ready to be condemned, that contained about forty old single trailers on extra wide and deep lots, more than half were vacant and he purchased the entire park and even the occupied ones, and had sped up the process by giving the owners more than what the trailers were really worth. After they were vacated he demolished them all, sold them as scrap metal, then purchased several nearby dated frame homes in the same neighborhood, nearly half were vacant and many were bank owned since the neighborhood had now became a less than desirable area to live in. They numbered close to around eighteen that bordered the park and were within the perimeter of the four streets that also bordered a portion of the fairly large trailer park and quickly demolished them all. Now he had more than doubled the size of the new and improved park he envisioned and would soon start building. He upgraded and installed all new sewage and water lines by replacing them, removed and replaced the interior roadways and made many improvements such as, by adding street lamps and curbs and placed all the electrical, telephone and cable services underground. He then brought in eighty luxury double wide's, or rather manufacture homes turning it into a very upscale and very desirable neighborhood to live in. Most had car ports, and decks, and Carl really removed the trailer park feeling that had existed before as he added trees, shrubs and had the entire property beautifully landscaped. He sold it like you would condos, and more than tripled his profit over his initial investment. Carl was now on a roll, the project was so successful and beautiful that it had write ups in the home sections of several of the local newspapers for many weeks as an example of the many new trends in living. He just couldn't stop now and looked around and attended even more auctions and bided on several more large foreclosed properties and soon he had an inventory of houses and apartment building as he now decided to operate it as a separate business and became a landlord operating under several different names for some of the larger properties but under one management company. His broker's license allowed him to make more money since he didn't have to pay any outside agents, but did end up hiring a managing broker and a couple of aspiring associates because he was just too busy and the company now had grown far beyond any of his wildest expectations. He had a six to fifteen month turn around between buying, fixing and selling the properties he acquired most of the time, and because he had all the materials and manpower available, the work progressed fairly quickly and was professionally done. Carl soon started a separate roofing company with its own dedicated crews and equipment just for his own houses, apartments and office buildings and now covered everything that could be done to a home and this really added even more quality to his rehabs since he was now the plumber, electrician, roofer and air conditioning man, then finally the broker, salesman or landlord and all the profits were his and soon had an even larger revolving business bank account that allowed for him to pursue even more lucrative and larger business opportunities.

Carl now ventured into the larger and more commercial and industrial type of properties. With even larger profits and soon was one of the top three companies in his line of work in the surrounding area, and eventually the state.

# Two

Carl continued to invest in and rehab considerably many more properties, residential, multifamily and now commercial and with his air conditioning, heating, electrical, plumbing, roofing, rehabbing and real estate business. He was now making over a million dollars a year in profits. He decided to sell his third home after he found one he thought would better suit the lifestyle he wanted to pursue over all the others he had lived in before after its completion. This house was located on a full acre of land and the neighborhood was much more upscale and was in a well-established and very quiet suburban area and the location was even more private due to the large acreage of all the surrounding homes. It was in the very early stages of being built when he found it; the complete foundation had yet been poured and only some of the underground infrastructure was in place since it was in the very early stages of being laid out before the complete foundation could be poured and completed. It was put up for sale after the people who were going to have it built wanted out of the contract before the contractor even started because of some sudden change of heart or a sudden change in their finances. He could never really find out why they suddenly decided to sell and very quickly moved out of state, and listed it as unfinished but under contract which allowed for him to have some special features added after talking to, and then signing a contract with both the architect and the building contractor when he let the seller out of their binding agreement. Carl was able to purchase the land from them, the sellers at cost by letting them off the hook for the construction cost since they had signed a binding agreement with the builder. Carl was a shrewd negotiator and had all the parties at the negotiation table and soon was in possession of the property. He negotiated to have the contractor purchase all his building materials through him if he wanted to be able to complete the contract which was very profitable for him and finish what he was about to start, plus it allowed Carl to ensure only quality materials were used and upgraded several items that were part of the main structure. It was going to be the only new home to be built in the area of stately and very established homes with the last and newest one in the area being built only seven years earlier. It sat on a slight hill and was built with a steel and concrete structure that allowed it to have very large, open and expansive spaces with five bedrooms and six full baths, with two half baths and Carl had the architect eliminate one of the large bed rooms and combine the space into the master bedroom, so now the master bedroom was much larger than what he had in his two previous homes and was equal in total size to a small apartment. The entire home was very large in total square footage. The master bedroom would have been larger than most bedrooms before the changes were made and would have accommodated a king size bed and a couch and some chairs, but now the bedroom was extra, extra large for an above average size bedroom. Carl had it designed with a wet bar and now having an even larger walk-in closet and the master bathroom increased in size with an extra-large walk in shower, pedestal bathtub, walk-in bathtub, sauna, dual vanity, bidet, toilet and urinal. There were two other bed rooms that were larger than most, each with its own walk-in closet and with their own large private bathrooms, and each one would be considered oversized, and the forth bedroom, the smallest was over the extra deep and large attached four car garage with a large bathroom and an extra-large walk-in wall closet, it seemed more suited for a child or servant only because it was the smallest bedroom in the house, but would still be considered extra-large by average bedroom standards. The kitchen was very convenient and large, having an eat in counter with several stylish high chairs, built in ovens, refrigerators, freezers and a work island with a cook top and a double sink, one of two and a cozy breakfast nook area with a large built in wrap around booth and table, the home had a very large living and dining rooms and all the rooms were extra-large spaces and were very open with high vaulted angular ceilings in some rooms, extra-large windows, skylights and it even had a large elevator to all three levels. There was a large open area in the center of the home, a small well laid out courtyard that all the rooms were arraigned around with a walk around balcony on the second floor where all the bedrooms were located. Carl had a California king bedroom suite along with a full size living room suite with several extra matching pieces in his bedroom along with a large 110 inch flat screen television mounted on one wall. There was also a refrigerator behind the built-in wet bar with four bar stools and a lighted mirror wall behind it. He had another area off to one side with his large desk, a built in book case in one corner near the balcony door to the outside cantilever porch thirty feet above the ground overlooking the front entrance and driveway. It also had a deep basement with a high nine foot ceiling and a very large thirty-five foot built-in wet bar with over a dozen stools, a refrigerator and eventually Carl had a couple billiards tables installed. Other than the kitchen which had the counter top with six high backed stools, the breakfast nook on the side, there was the large laundry room with twin extra-large capacity washers and dryers. There was also a separate and spacious mud room leading from the attached garage. And outside was a natural gas powered backup generator for emergencies. Carl didn't worry about furniture to much yet because he was still contemplating how long he would be here, but was getting tired of moving so often. He hadn't yet fully decided if this was his last house or not, but was pretty sure it was because he had so much input as to it design; it was him and he felt really comfortable here.

Very soon after his new home was completed and he had moved in, several of his new neighbors came by and wanted to welcome him to the neighborhood. They were also really curious about this new extremely large, energy efficient home that had just been built with its beautiful ultra-modern exterior appearance, and very appealing and sexy style, with its metal roof covered with sky lights, large windows and solar panels, and everyone wondered who really lived here. They were all well to do, and were mostly professionals and a group of successful business people and a few were blue collar people just like himself who had worked themselves into a higher tax bracket but were still very down to earth folks. Carl was happy to be so warmly welcomed, and gave the first few curious visitors a quick tour of his new home. They were soon inviting him to some of their social gatherings and neighborhood events which he did happily attend, and very much enjoyed making new friends and it gave him an opportunity to pass out some of his business cards and also gathered many of theirs.

His new neighbors had a neighborhood association and Carl was invited to join and soon became a full-fledged member just like everyone else who lived in the neighborhood. Some times when he drove one of his vans home he would leave it in the driveway as advertisement and have his lunch which he enjoyed doing sometimes. The home had an extra deep four car garage and Carl eventually began parking his old auto inside. Every now and then his office would receive phone calls from his neighbors for work they wanted or needed done and Carl would always send one of his best crews to do the work. His secretary Mary Sue always informed him when someone from his neighborhood called. All his businesses ventures were doing very well and soon he changed his primary business location for the third time. This time he moved into a much larger building that had an extremely large warehouse attached with seventy five dock doors and more than enough space for deliveries and plenty of storage space and there was also an exceptionally large two story attached office building where several companies had once been located at before. Carl purchased the entire eighty five acre site at below market value but still it was close to two million dollars since the original company that owned it had closed, then eventually went into bankruptcy and then had to sell all their assets off, some like this location cheaply because both buildings were in need of serious rehabbing and needed major upgrading and repairs to make them viable again. The location was ideal for his business and located not far from the major retail and business strips in the area and major highways and interstates and sat at the edge of a major industrial park and also had a rail spur leading to the building which would enhance his business even more for massive bulk deliveries. Carl, before moving his operations in stripped the office building down and completely did a total upgrade of all the utilities which was one of the reasons the prior occupants had moved out. The warehouse only needed the lighting and break areas along with the washrooms modernized and that didn't take any time and was minor compared to the office building portion of the property and allowed him to move his materials before he actually moved his office which worked out well. The office building was thirty years old and was cutting edge for its time, but time had passed it by as Carl now brought it up to date and beyond as he remodeled completely both levels even though he only needed a portion of the downstairs, which accounted for about a third of the entire available office space on the ground floor for all of his office operations which he was soon going to separate and operate independently, at least on paper. Soon after he opened the new location he bought out another small regional electrical supplier and consolidated all of their operations at the new location and still had more room to spare even after locating and reorganizing all of his various operations there. He had a larger and even better organized office space than ever before, and equipped it with the latest in business technology, with printers large enough to print blue prints for some of his expanding operations and had more space than he would ever need.

Since him and Mary Sue Anderson, his now very long time secretary and trusted personal confidant had along with him handled most of the ordering, pricing, and purchasing alone in the past. He after discussing with Mary Sue decided to hire a small efficient staff of qualified females. He along with Mary did all the interviews together and soon had assembled a small and very competent professional office staff. Now he didn't have to do all the work as his operations became even more efficient especially after moving. He placed Mary Sue in complete charge, giving her a company car and a generous pay raise; she was the highest paid employee in the company after him as he soon created a wholly owned private corporation and became the chief executive officer. She was then given the title of chief financial officer and office manager as she supervised and oversaw the entire office staff of seven other women. Carl had a few more employees, close to fifty as his operations grew and began spending almost all of his time now in the office overseeing his busy operation. He had separated the various departments and operated them now as separate companies basically on paper; they still consisted of roofing, electrical, plumbing, air conditioning and heat, rehabbing and real estate. Carl would still go out and survey all of the very large jobs prior to signing contracts for the work to be performed, until he began designating more of those duties to John Roberts who was his very first employee, and knew all the jobs and how Carl wanted things managed and now had his own office, a company car and was paid the same as Mary Sue. John held the title of chief of operations and now both John and Mary actually ran the entire operation as he now just oversaw more of the all-around daily operations. His business now was more efficient and thriving as he created several new positions and one was a new warehouse supervisors position and was in charge of all the warehouse operations and directed the five employees who worked there full time loading and unloading trucks, unloading the rail cars, stocking materials and handling inventory. They also managed and stocked the vast and varied abundance of materials on hand as he also became a major distributer of air conditioning and heating equipment, plumbing supplies and electrical for many smaller outfits and independent contractors and soon opened and operated a walk in supply facility in a portion of the extremely large warehouse, which soon turned out to be an entirely new operation all by its self. He was very happy with what he had accomplished and could now spent more time away from work as he slowly began decorating his newly completed home and soon decided this was his final move as he shopped more for large decorative items to fill the vast spaces in his large roomy home.

Carl still didn't have a girlfriend and some of his neighbors introduced him to some very nice single women but they didn't seem at all attracted to him or he to them and he really didn't care very much at this point in his life anyway. Some were real phonies and thought they were better than a lot of other people or even really stuck up. The one thing Carl did seem to notice was that the more expensive the neighborhood the more out of touch some of the residents seemed to be with the reality's and struggles in other people's lives around them sometimes. He just gave up thinking he would ever find anyone who would ever truly satisfy him mentally let lone physically, and stopped looking and figured it wouldn't happen until its time, just like much of everything else that had ever happened in his life that held any real meaning. He figured the perfect woman for him would want to show some interest in him first before he would even be bothered; he wasn't chasing anyone, except the next job or home re-hab.

One very pleasant early summer day, Carl decided to leave work early and on his way home decided he needed to stop by one of the local grocery stores and pick up a few needed items and just wanted to look around since grocery shopping was one enjoyable pass time for him. He figured while shopping he might catch some sales, since you really never know what you might find, or even run across. After entering and getting a shopping cart, Carl used the sanitary wipes by the entrance door and cleaned the cart handle off. Carl then proceeded to start looking around the fresh produce section since it was right at the entrance and soon had gathered a few items since he really liked to cook and found it relaxing before choosing several more items he had on his short list. Carl liked buying fresh vegetables and eating as healthy as possible and after several minutes shopping his attention to shopping was distracted in the direction of a woman who had just entered the busy store. He happen to noticed her because of her being very slim an almost anorexic looking, but was still a very attractive woman with a fair but slight olive completion. She was wearing a very long, thin and very worn cotton dress down almost to her slim ankles with a pair of very worn out flat shoes, she had very long and curly but almost straight dark brown hair tied in a ponytail. It wasn't often you would see someone as poorly dressed as she was having such a very pretty face, a little gaunt but clean, clear and blemish free and she wore no makeup, but with a dejected look on her face. Carl tried hard not to stare, it was her seemingly poor and frail appearance that had caught his eye as he turned away and continued looking for the fresh vegetables on his list and had just found the last fresh items when an older couple who passed near the slim woman made a very disparaging comment about her and they were loud enough to be heard by several other people shopping nearby and the comment which would have been very upsetting to anyone, but was specifically directed toward her almost made her cry as she wiped her now very moist eyes with the back of her hand, everyone around who witnessed the incident could tell it very much hurt her feelings. Carl didn't know what had possessed him to say anything to the young woman, as she approached in his direction and coming closer, when she did he spoke to her. He looked at her and smiled, and told her, she needed to smile because she was much to pretty to have such a forlorn look on her very pretty face and also told her to ignore what the very rude older couple had said as they passed by her. She looked at him and tried hard to smile back without crying as Carl looked in her pretty face and could see the anguish in her beautiful eyes and asked if he could do anything for her. In a low and very soft voice, said no thank you sir, but thank you anyway I can manage. Carl turned back around after wishing her to have a great day, and continued on with his shopping.

As he was now finished with the fresh produce section he continued making his way into the bakery section before then slowly walking up and down another couple of aisles and finding some of the other items on his list and would soon be finished with this shopping adventure. Then he again saw the thin woman as she approached from the opposite direction of the same aisle he was now in. She now approached Carl and said sir; please sir, as he turned and faced her as she asked if she could speak to him. Carl after turning around and looking at her, said yes madam. She said sir, as she just came right out and asked Carl if he would punish her. He was so taken aback by this, her very bold and strange request, and was so caught off guard that he just said to her no way, never ever. She asked him if he had a moment so she could please explain. Carl said yes please do explain. She did and began telling him about her husband of almost fourteen years and how he had died suddenly and she was now a widow, and was very much all alone now. He had made her into his servant and had been his slave now for more than ten years and was lost and very confused and needed some guidance and especially someone to talk to and also someone to discipline her and couldn't explain her reasons now for choosing him, except that he had shown her some compassion and concern a few minutes earlier. She only had two items in a small hand held basket while Carl had a shopping cart. She told Carl she was very serious, and this wasn't a joke and really wanted and needed someone to talk to because she didn't know what else to do. As he looked at her more closely he began noticing she was bra less as her long nipples pressed against the thin material and began to stiffen as she spoke to him about her situation. She was wearing the well-worn and very thin with too many washings cotton print dress you could almost see through, and was the reason she had drawn the ire of the older couple earlier since she wore nothing else. She asked Carl if she could please shop with him in a very pleading manor and looking like she might drop to her knees and begin crying at any minute. He told her yes, she could, as they proceeded to go down the remaining aisles together and passed another woman, who was also very outspoken as they passed by, she also made a very derogatory comment under her breath and sneered which this reaction from this particular woman began to also upset Carl. It wasn't long before Carl was finished with his shopping. Carl had the fairly young woman check out before him only with the five items she had purchased, which was a small jar of peanut butter, a half loaf of bread, a small jar of jelly, and two small cans of pork and beans. She was waiting patiently as Carl paid for his groceries, and as he glanced over to where she stood waiting, could now see what had brought all the unwanted attention to her. You could almost see through the thin dress she wore as she was standing by the window with the sun behind her as it outlined her shapely but slim figure and gave her the appearance of almost being nude. He finished checking out as they then headed for the parking lot together. Carl now asked the woman her name, she said it was Betty, Mrs. Betty Johnson, as Carl introduced himself and asked where her car was parked. Then she told him she didn't have a car and had walked several blocks from the apartment complex where she lived, and that her husband had wrecked their car when he died in the one car accident.

After placing his groceries into the trunk of his vehicle, he asked Betty if she was hungry. She very quickly answered, yes sir, and Carl then placed her bag in the back seat of his car and suggested they walk the short distance over to the fast food restaurant that was located on the other side of the parking lot. They walked together and entered as Carl held the door for her and said to her, to order whatever she wanted, and said he would gladly pay for it as they placed their orders together and were given a number to place on their table. They proceeded to find a booth to sit at as they now waited for their orders and Betty almost started to explain her dire situation as an employee brought there order to their table, and removed the large order number card from the table. Carl was very skeptical of this Betty and her debased character as he then asked her to please explain to him her situation.

She started out by telling him that her late husband was driving home one evening after work and was extremely drunk after stopping off and having a few drinks. He left the tavern and on his way home ran into a tree at a high rate of speed and dying shortly afterwards at the scene and totaling the automobile and that had happened a little over three months earlier. He had made her his slave, she was forced to become his willing submissive, she had to serve him as his slave almost the entire time they were married. Now that he was deceased, she was very frightened because of the lifestyle he had placed her in and didn't know what to do or who to talk to, she had no friends or relatives and he had kept her almost completely isolated from other people. Betty ate like she hadn't eaten in several days or even weeks as she consumed every little crumb from the hamburger and French fries as she consumed the drink. Carl asked her all about that as he observed her eating habits. Said she ate only what the master had allowed her to eat. Carl thought that was why she was so very thin, and almost anorexic in appearance. She again asked Carl if he would now punish and whip her because she had broken all of her master's rules. Carl looked at her in stunned disbelief and asked what rules were those. She explained how she had taken the money he had left at home to buy some food since he was the one who did all the shopping as she was made to follow him around the store and then carry the bags to the car, then inside as he just watched her. Carl observed the wedding ring she still wore and told her that now she didn't needed a master; she was free to do whatever she wanted. But then Betty suddenly asked him if he would become her new master. Carl wasn't at all very interested in having someone like Betty around as he explained to her she didn't need anyone around to mistreat her any longer and wasn't interested in being anyone's master, but would have to see if he could help her or get her some help and only because she seemed so despondent and in need of some type of assistance. Carl said he would help her get on her feet and see what could be done for her since he began to feel really sorry for her. Before they had finished eating Betty looked him in his eyes with all sincerity and said she would be a good slave and do whatever he wanted. Betty soon finished her food and shortly after, Carl finished his. He asked her if she was ready to go, and she said yes sir master. Carl frowned when she said that, and told her he wasn't anyone master and didn't intend to be, ever. They exited the restaurant and walked to his car. He opened the front passenger door for her as she stood by the back door looking coy and wanting to ride in the back seat. Carl asked her why, she said slaves always rode in back; it's where worthless slaves were to sit. Carl said get in front now, and said it in a very commanding voice, and she quickly obeyed. Carl asked her where she lived as she directed him to a nearby apartment complex almost a mile away where she stayed.

It wasn't very far by auto but was a good long walk otherwise as they soon arrived at a mid-sized apartment complex that had an almost park like setting as she directed him around to the side she lived on. They stepped out of the car as she carried her small bag and led him to a second floor unit. There on the door, was taped an eviction notice. Betty took the notice down and unlocked the door as they entered. It was a very large but sparsely furnished, one bedroom apartment, with very cheap and old furniture that had long ago seen much better days. Betty quickly showed Carl around as he asked her about the notice, she handed it to him and he read it, the rent was now two months pass due and Carl asked her who paid the rent. She said her master did, her now deceased husband, who Carl now realized she never called him by his name. Carl asked her to give him the check book and all the records and paper work that the master had used. She went to the bedroom and soon returned with a very large big brown envelope, the type used for storage or in place of a briefcase, with an attached string that was tied; it was filled with all sorts of documents and important papers as its accordion shape was stretched to the limit. Carl dumped it all out on the large empty wooden kitchen table and pulled up one of the three very hard wooden chairs, and sat down and started sorting out the various unopened envelopes as he began looking through the many documents and soon found the old apartment lease and a new one as he continued looking and soon found the monthly amount. Then looking at the check book ledger for the checking account, he soon realized as he checked, the amounts in the check book were not up to date since it appeared the last entry was a couple days before her late husband's demise. Harold was his name as Carl saw the names on the checks, Mr. and Mrs. Harold and Betty Johnson. Carl also found several bank statements in envelopes which hadn't been opened for the past three months since he died and quickly checked the balances and brought the check book up to date. He turned and asked Betty to sit down since she just stood looking down at him with a very curious and overly anxious look on her face. Carl asked her to make out the rent checks, for the past due monthly amounts for the rent. She did know how to make out a check which proved to Carl she was completely competent and not totally stupid or helpless. When she finished filling out the checks, he decided they should take these over to the rental office so she wouldn't get evicted and end up homeless. He walked over with her to the apartment complex office and had her to pay the rent and then they both returned to the apartment. As Carl returned and continued to further look through the documents he saw at least her name was on all the important documents and accounts which made things so much simpler and easier to put in order. There had been one large deposit made a couple weeks after her husband's death which looked like it came from some sort of insurance policy, the amount was for $34,642.15 dollars and had been deposited into the checking account and appeared to come from the funeral home that had taken care of the body, then he found their bill and it showed she had received the remainder from a forty thousand dollar policy. Carl also found pass due electric and gas bills as he opened all the unopened envelopes, and had her make out checks for the utilities also, found some postage stamps and prepared them for the mailbox, and as he looked further, found a couple more insurance policies payable to her in case of his and even two on her plus the police report on Harold's accident. There were two she needed to cash in and found several certified copies of the death certificates for her husband Harold and contacted the insurance companies on his cell phone and informed them of his death, fortunately for her the premiums were paid directly from the checking account. Her husband had four other insurance policies, one for $100,000.00 and a second for $50,000.00 as Carl put in motion the process for her to collect on them. The other two were on Betty, both had been taken out at the same time as the two on Harold and all were initiated long before Betty's pregnancy. She had been pregnant at one time and wondered just what had happened since there weren't any signs of children around the apartment. He turned to her and told her what he had just done. She asked him if he would be her master now. Carl looked at her stunned, and couldn't understand her mind set as he told her no, absolutely not, that she didn't any longer need a master. He continued putting her banking records in some type of order and realized she really did need some kind of help. Betty again asked if he would be her master. Carl now figured he had placed himself in a real trick bag and turned to her and noticed the tears in her eyes as he told her no again. Betty dropped to her knees and begged him please. Carl looked at her and said I will be your master only if you are obedient, and it seemed that was all she was really concerned about. Carl then asked her when her husband died who made the arrangements for his funeral since she seemed so incapable of making any type of funeral arrangements. Betty wiped the tears from her face with the back of her hand and said two people from his job came over, a man and a woman from the warehouse where he worked. She said when they saw how upset and distraught she was they made all the funeral arraignments for her, and said she attended a very small service for him. It was only her and a couple of his coworkers in attendance since his sister had passed the year before and was his last known living relative as far as she knew. Carl asked if he was buried and where. She replied they cremated him and then gave her the ashes. Carl asked what she did with them. Said she dumped his ashes in the trash. Carl didn't even bother asking her why. He looked around the apartment and found it was very clean and spotless. When he checked the kitchen cabinets, he was shocked at how empty they were. Other than what she had purchased today there was basically nothing in the kitchen or the refrigerator for her to eat, except some salt and pepper and a small bottle of olive oil.

He turned to her and told her to hold out her hands, she did as he told her to remove the wedding ring she wore. Told her it was her old master's ring and now she was free and didn't need a master any longer. He asked Betty why was there a large dog cage in the living room with a blanket inside near the sliding glass door to the porch and no dog. She said that was her cage where master had kept her when he was tired of her or wanted to punish her and sometimes poked her with a broom stick. She asked if master was ready for her to serve him as she now stood, turned and quickly walked into the bedroom and soon returned naked with her dog collar on and a leash attached and knelt down before Carl and handed him a heavy leather strap, and said, please master. Carl was shocked and stunned at the same time while being aroused by her sudden action, and asked her where did she get this from, she stood as Carl followed her into the bedroom. She opened a large drawer in the large cheap dresser in the small bedroom; it was filled with all the various items her husband had used on her. He looked shocked and amazed as he pulled out another cruel looking leather strap, another longer leather leash and observed that the drawer was filled with all sorts of cuffs, whips, anal plugs, dildos, pumps, clamps of various sizes, suction tubes and devices and which contained a vast assortment of other cruel looking bondage equipment. He looked around the bed room and the bed was neatly made, and next to the bed on the floor, was a very thin an old worn mattress along with an old pillow without a case, and a worn and thin blanket with holes in it, he asked her where did she slept, as she now pointed to the floor, and she said only the master could sleep in the bed.

He asked Betty to please put her dress back on; she refused as he returned to the living room. She followed him as he sat down again and she now stood in front of him, then knelt down in front of him looking up and said please as he looked at her slim but still beautiful body. She was very slender, her brunette hair was very long down her bony back almost to her waist, her skin was smooth and soft and remarkably flawless and her vaginal area was very clean and showed hardly any signs of ever growing any hair. He told her to turn around and bend over as he looked at her rectum. He could tell she had anal sex as he asked her to stand and then sit in the lounge chair which she was very hesitant to do because she said it was the masters' chair as Carl told her sit and spread her legs open as he looked at her vagina up close. Carl could see she had been clamped in the past by the length and size of her large long vaginal lips close up. She had truly been a slave to her deceased husband. He told her to stand and looked at her breasts which at one time were much larger and fuller as the areolas were large and the nipples very long from some sort of vacuum stretching of some sorts, and had seen it done in some s&m videos. He asked her if she still wanted to be spanked, to which she replied yes, please master, that she wanted to serve her new master and needed a hard spanking to prove she was worthy. Carl tried very hard not to become aroused as he was having a massive hard on, he suppressed his carnal feelings, but then again how often would you have a strange woman ask you to punish her and stand before you in the buff as he distracted his thoughts by asking her some more questions. He asked if her past master kept or took any pictures of her to which she said, yes sir master. He asked her to please get them as she went and removed two very large and thick photo albums from under the old end table next to the much worn couch. Carl wanted to look thru them and after a few moments, he reached for and pulled the leash on her neck and had her kneel with her hands and fingers locked behind her head. She was still a very beautiful woman, you could really see it, she just needed to be feed regular and loved as Carl did a quick scan through the photo album of Betty in restraints, in her cage and bent over a chair with whip and whelp marks all over her body, hanging, tied, clamped, whipped and even some of her preforming oral sex on her master, some with the large anal plugs inserted and dildos, blindfolded and chained and tied in different and very cruel positions. She was more or less being abused most of the time and her husband had some photos of her outside tied up to trees and walking her like a dog, crawling and had several with a noose around her neck. Carl wondered if this is what she truly wanted as he turned and looked at her still in the position he had left her in, kneeling with her hands behind her head as he looked into her eyes and began speaking to her.

Carl asked her if she felt comfortable being in this position, she replied whatever the master wanted of her. He asked her who was her master, and she replied you are now sir. He asked her if there were any videos of her that her husband had made since Carl had noticed a video camera in some of the photos as he had glanced through the photo album, and she replied, yes sir master. Carl asked her to get them as she went to a cabinet and pulled out a large thick book you could keep about fifty or so CDs in and handed the very heavy book to Carl and returned to kneeling before him with her hands behind her head. Carl looked at her and hooked the leash to her collar, told her to get down like a dog which she immediately did, as he then led her around the apartment before sitting on the cheap couch and having her again kneel before him, he pulled her to him and touched her for the very first time, as he felt her face and had her open her mouth as he looked inside and her teeth were clean and white, besides being more than slightly under weight she seemed to be in very good health which was the next thing he asked her about. Betty said her husband and master took her to the doctor every year for a checkup, and the last one was a month before his untimely death. Carl asked her if she wanted that spanking, to which she happily replied, yes please master, and said she really wanted it badly, to please her new master and it would prove to him she was worthy. Carl pulled the leash and had her bend over his lap and spread her legs as he placed his left hand on her shoulders holding her in place as he smacked her ass cheeks, alternating as he did so and after about ten smacks her cheeks began to redden some. Carl had noticed from the photo album she had endured so much worse and even more severe punishments than what he had just inflicted on her, as she now began to beg for more and much harder.

Carl reached over for the leather strap she had brought when she first appeared before him nude. He held it and began to spank her posterior as it reddened even more with each blow before he pulled her up, and looked into her face. Her face now had the look of complete satisfaction. He asked her what she had to say for herself and she replied thank you master. Carl stood and pulled her up then felt her now between her legs as she held her arms behind her back in a very submissive pose like he had seen in some videos as she now became very excited and moist as he continued feeling her as he asked her if she wanted to climax. She said yes please master may I come, and as he said yes you can, she had a most violent organism as her knees now bent and her entire body shook violently. Carl asked her after a couple minutes what do you say, and she said out of breath, thank you master. Carl was now very excited with this exhibition of true servitude and decided he would make Betty his submissive after all, but for now she would have to remain here until he figured out just what to do with her. He would take the videos and pictures home with him and further examine them, but first he would make her clean herself up. He asked her for the masters set of keys, told her to get them as she again went to the bed room and retrieved his set from one of the dresser drawers as Carl followed her. He made her kneel in the bed which she was extremely hesitant to do, but did so after he smacked her ass, and told her to bend over with her ass up head down and arms besides her ankles. Carl opened the drawer where he found all the various cuffs and restraint items and removed a pair of cuffs, and decided to cuff Bettie's wrist and ankles together with the wide leather cuffs using the clamps he found in the drawer. She still had the collar on and the leash was still attached as he reached for the leash and pulled it between her legs causing her butt to raise up higher and letting it lie on the bed as he returned to the drawer and removed a large anal plug and also found some lubricant which he liberally applied before slowly working it into her upturned anus, once it was fully inserted he found a penis shaped vibrating dildo, he lubricated her up and slowly inserted it into her now very moist vagina and slowly worked it inside of her until it was fully inserted and turned it on low.

Carl then left the bedroom and returned to the kitchen, sitting down as he looked carefully at the photos in the first album and looked at Bettie over the preceding years. She had been trained slowly over time and the book was in chronological order, and as the years passed she was taken to more extreme limits as her husband subjected her to more extensive and even more very humiliating and degrading treatments. She was truly a submissive and Carl would feel bad now if he left her on her own or to someone else who would really take advantage and abuse her even more harshly after what had occurred in her past, and then there were the insurance monies which would really make her a prime target of abuse. He had walked into a situation as much by accident or guided on purpose for some unexplained reason, just trying to be Mr. Nice guy and had placed himself into a position of now being a master or guardian and had never wanted or expected anything like this to ever happen to him. After about ten minutes he returned to the bed room where he had left her, and Betty was now having continuous orgasmic spasms as she shook uncontrollably as her slender body was racked with unending pleasure. Carl now began working the dildo back and forth before slowly removing it. Then he began slowly working the butt plug back and forth until he removed it and then inserting the vibrating dildo in her anus and working it in and out as he reached around and played with her now very enlarged and long clitoris causing her to climax repeatedly several more times before he removed it and laying it on top of the dresser. He pushed her over onto her side and looked into her face, which was filled with the look of intense pleasure and satisfaction as she gasps for her breath. Carl unhooked her ankles from her wrist and just let her lie there panting as she stretched out before he took the leash and pulled her up to her feet and asking her what do you say, with a bated breath, said thank you master, then he told her to crawl as he led her around the large apartment before leading her to the bathroom where he told her to stand as he removed the collar, leash and cuffs, and ordered her to shower and wash her anus and vagina, she said yes sir master. While she bathed he looked in the closet and found she didn't hardly have any clothes, but found her husband had an overly abundant amount of nice clothing. She only had four dresses including the very thin one she had on today and two others that were too old and were very worn out also and were closer to being rags. And one black tube dress which hung neatly from a hanger. It appeared almost new and undamaged as Carl wondered about it. Then he looked for her shoes, she had the worn out flats she had worn today and there was a pair of fairly new black high heels and that was the extent of her wardrobe. Then he remembered several photos of her in the dress looking very sexy but thin with the collar and leash attached. Carl returned to the bathroom and told her to wash her hair also, she said yes sir master and when she finished, she began drying off as she again appeared before him. He asked her to place a towel on the bed before telling her to lie down. He had noticed the small bottle of olive oil in the kitchen and returned and began massaging her with the oil as he closely began inspecting her very slender body.

By massaging her he got to feel her body and examine her much more closely. Her toes were straight and they had no polish and her toe nails were clean and neatly trimmed and the same held true for her hands with long slender fingers with short, clean and trimmed nails. He could see no physical flaws in her and had her stand and brush her damp hair out and use the blow dryer he found that she had until it was dry and had her apply some of the oil to her long beautiful and thick hair as she brushed it. Carl was a passionate person as he held her face in both his hands and kissed her on the lips, and then she began crying. He looked at her, and she looked back at him with very submissive and pleading eyes and reached out and grabbed him, hugging him as she just continued crying. Carl had to pry her away and then asked if she had any jewelry. She opened a drawer and removed a small box and opened it. There were only a couple pairs of earrings and he chose a tiered pair with a matching necklace which was all she really had and told her to put them on and the black dress and asked if she had any stockings, she looked in the same drawer and there were only two pair and the newest ones was a pair of crotch less panty hose and they were still in the package which he told her to put on along with the high heels. He made her stand and look in the mirror at herself, before asking her if she had any make up and all she had was some face cream which Carl then said never mind. When she finished dressing she was very slender, but beautiful and Carl asked her if she had a purse and she pulled out of the same drawer two of them, and one was black. Carl looked at her and told her to put her keys into the black purse, which she did and took her by the hand and led her outside of the apartment, locking the door and then they walked to his auto, he opened the door for her as he drove her to a nice restaurant he knew of nearby where they entered and were soon seated in a comfortable booth.

Carl looked at Bettie and she had tears in her pretty brown eyes as he sat back and just looked at her. He asked her why was she crying, she began by telling him it was because she felt happy inside now, that she had a new master who would love her. Carl said what makes you think I love you or want to even be your master. She said because he had spanked her and if a master loved his slave he would punish her because he loved her. Carl thought how fucked up a thought that was, but now he would be committed to watching out for this poor and very emotionally needy piece of humanity called Betty. The waiter came and Carl ordered for both of them after checking with her if there was anything she couldn't eat, to which she replied no. The waiter returned bringing them the glasses of wine he had ordered. He looked at Betty and knew all he had to do was command her to do whatever he wanted. He asked Betty what do you want out of life, and she replied to serve you Master Carl. This was the first time she referred to him by his name. He asked her if there was anything she wouldn't do if he told her to do it, to which she replied no sir; said she was her master's property and was here to serve him. Carl asked her if he told her to stand up and strip would she do it, she answered if that is what the master desired of her as she began to stand up, Carl quickly said sit down. She sat back down and Carl was amazed by her complete and total obedience. Their food came and he asked her to please eat which she began to do. She ate with poise and grace and it was obvious she had been brought up with manners and wondered how she had managed to become so utterly and completely submissive.

After dinner he asked her if she wanted any descrt and she said if her master wanted her to have some and when the waiter returned he ordered for them both again. He brought the dessert and she ate it. Carl paid the bill and they soon departed the restaurant. He opened the car door for her and she got in and he ordered her to pull her dress up which she did as he reached and felt between her thin thighs and told her to open them wide which she did, as he played with her and she began to get moist very quickly and once he started driving told her to pull her dress down from the top exposing her breast as he reached over and squeezed and pulled a nipple hard making her squirm before telling her to pull it back up. Soon they were back at her apartment and exited the auto and reentered her apartment again. Once they were inside Betty asked him if master was satisfied and pleased with her, and Carl responded yes so far. She asked if master wanted her, that she was here to please her master. Carl told her to undress and put her clothes away for the next time he would take her out. She replaced her clothes and jewelry and returned to the living room nude and knelt before Carl with her head bowed.

# Three

Carl sat and looked at her kneeling down before him, looking head down in a very submissive pose with her arms folded behind her back and remembered that her lease would be up in a couple of months when he had quickly went through her documents looking for the monthly rent amount. He asked her if there was a suit case available, she raised her head, and looked up at him with a dispirited look on her pretty face and said that master had a brand new set. Carl asked her to get them and place them on the bed. She stood and returned to the bedroom as he followed as she went to the closet and opened the sliding door and quickly removed a large suitcase and placed it on the bed as instructed. Carl opened it and there was another large bag inside of the largest bag as he took it out and opened the second bag and inside of it there were two smaller carryon bags inside, this was a brand new set that had never been used and still had the store price tags on the handle. Carl told her to leave them on the bed and said he was going home and would come back tomorrow. Betty quickly fell down on her knees, reaching out as she grabbed his legs wrapping her arms around them, looking up and begging him to please don't leave her alone. She pleaded with him as she looked up crying as tears ran down her pretty face as she begged and pleaded with him, please Master Carl, please don't leave me alone as her whole body began trembling and shaking as she pleaded with him, please master Carl, please. After several minutes Carl then told her to stand up; as she did she was shaking as if she was truly terrified that something terrible would happen to her. Carl told her to start packing as he pulled out the drawer with all the bondage equipment in it, completely removing it and just dumped the contents into the smaller of the two large suit cases and told her to place all of her clothing and personal belongings and whatever into the larger suitcase. Betty was now extremely anxious to leave with him as she hurriedly placed everything she owned inside the suitcase, when she finished which it didn't take very long with the few meager belonging she had, he took her large brown envelope and placed it into one of the smaller bags along with the photo albums and the video disc case he placed in the second small bag, then had her roll up her bedding, the pillow, blanket and flat mattress. He asked her about a video camera which he had seen in the photographs as she quickly went and removed it from the closet which was in a carrying case along with a second camera case, which he opened and found a digital SLR inside as she returned to the closet and removed a large laptop in a carrying case along with a tripod. Carl told her to dress as she now didn't hesitate to put on the long dress she had worn earlier with the old flat shoes. He looked around and had her open all the drawers in the bedroom, as he also looked inside the closet before going to the living room and even the kitchen as he went around the apartment checking and making sure he had all of her papers and soon there were only her deceased husbands clothing and the cheap worn out furniture remaining along with an old analog television. He looked at her and held her head in both his hands and said to her, if she wasn't good or obedient, he would return her here to live alone. She looked at Carl and said she would be very obedient and very good as she sniffled and wiped the moisture on her face from her earlier tears. He told her he would see how well she worked out at keeping his house clean. She said thank you master Carl. Carl thought she at least knew what to say and when to say it, which meant she wasn't completely stupid. Together they headed downstairs to his auto and he could see Betty was more than anxious to leave here and probably would follow him wherever he went or even took her. As much as he was still very skeptical of her, he wondered just how she felt, so far she was very trusting of him being a good person as it just seemed like she would follow him anywhere.

He carried the smaller bags with the photos and documents downstairs and opened the trunk of his car and placing them inside, before returning and helping Betty carry the remaining suit cases downstairs before he returned to lock her apartment door. After placing all the bags in the car's trunk along with her mattress she stood by the car door now as he opened it from the inside. Betty quickly got inside with Carl and he shortly pulled off and fifty five minutes later pulled onto his long driveway. Betty sat in the car and had said absolutely nothing the entire time as he drove home. Carl pulled up and waited until the garage door opened, after he had pulled into the garage and closed the garage door he told her to get out. He began taking her bags out of the car and had her bring them to the back door where he had her wait until he took his groceries inside and had her stand by the back door until he finished putting them away. Carl had unintentionally started his master, slave relationship by having her wait by the backdoor until he finished putting away his groceries, when he finished and returned to the garage Betty was still standing where he had left her. He brought one of her bags inside and told her to follow with the rest of her stuff and had decided where she would stay in his large house. He took her upstairs along with all the bags from her apartment as they rode up on the elevator to the second floor and led her to the small empty bedroom over the garage. Carl said to her until he could decide if she was truly worthy to serve him, and until he decided how long she would be staying here she would sleep in here for now, he showed her the bathroom as Betty looked around and he told her she would have to keep his house clean at all times and failure to do so would result in her returning to living alone or even on the street. He asked her if she understood, she replied, yes sir master Carl. She unrolled her bed as it was now late in the afternoon leaving her in the bedroom and left to check on his house. He took the photo and videos albums along with the cameras and laptop to his bedroom and set it all by his desk and the case with bondage and restraint equipment to his closet. After undressing and taking a nice long warm shower and putting on some clean shorts, he fixed a drink and finally sat down and started to relax on his bedroom sofa, thinking about what the implications of having her here would mean and what else might follow. After a short while he went and sat at his desk and began going through Betty's documents again, this time more thoroughly and after an hour had put everything in much better order and more up to date and also had balanced her checking account much better and making sure he hadn't overlooked anything. They had mailed the overdue utility bills he had her make out checks for before leaving her apartment. He would soon contact a charity and have them remove the furniture and clothing from her apartment and then have her clean it up so she could get her security deposit back, then take her to social security and see what benefits she could claim and also update her bank accounts or open new ones since she seemed incapable of taking care of her personal business, and besides she had no means of transportation. While looking again at her documents is when he found an envelope he had over looked before. Inside it was a hand written note by Harold and had no date on it but stated he wasn't renewing the lease and was moving. It was addressed to the leasing agent and seemed very incomplete for some reason as it just ended abruptly without a date. Carl figured he wasn't finished when he started writing it as it seemed so unfinished but a joint saving account pass book and his passport were also inside and the bank book contained a tidy sum of $26 thousand dollars and some cents. He sat and thought again about what he had gotten himself into, and how this would all work out.

While he sat at his big desk he decided to turn on his computer and waited for it to boot up as he viewed much more closely the photo album her husband had put together over the years and started at the very beginning since he had complied a very thorough record over the many years they were married and found out she had become pregnant at one time, but something happened not long after the baby was born before his first birthday and remembered finding several birth certificates and a death certificate other than her husbands and pulled her documents back out and again looking. There were both of their birth certificates and the third one was for a child. The baby only lived eight months. Then Carl looked through the video disks and they all had dates written on them as well as being numbered in some type of sequence. Carl started with the oldest which was labeled number one, and placed it in his computer after it had booted up. It began with the happy couple on their wedding day and then on their honeymoon almost fourteen years earlier. The second, third and fourth disc showed even much happier times, but by the time he looked at the fifth disc it was four almost five years later when Betty was now pregnant, smiling and very happy, then the birth of a beautiful baby boy, when he was born they were so very happy, kissing and appeared to be the perfect family unit, there were about three more disc of the happy family before the last which was about three hours of the baby before it showed briefly some funeral footage and then a grave site with the baby's name on a head stone, Ronald H Johnson, and then the very distraught parents. Then there were more pictures after the baby's death and you could see Betty was far from being happy now. Harold, her husband appeared on camera, he was sitting down as he explained that they had been a very happy family, but because Betty was careless as a mother the baby had drown after leaving him alone in the bath tub for just a few minutes and explained how the fire department couldn't resuscitate the child, but he was taken to the hospital and the cause of death verified and a death certificate was then issued.

In the next disc, as Carl continued to follow them in sequence, Harold went on to explain how completely devastated he now felt and how he would never, or could ever forgive Betty for her down right careless act of sheer stupidity, and after being so very lucky to have become pregnant in the very first place, he could never forgive her. And now she couldn't have any more children. The doctors had said her having any more children was completely out of the question since this had been one very difficult pregnancy and they were very fortunate to have had such a very healthy child since she would never be able to conceive or give birth again because of a condition with her fallopian tubes where they collapsed. Harold went on to say that if she stayed with him and didn't leave now he would have to punish her every day for the rest of her natural born life and he was completely prepared to follow through with his promise. He also stated she had no other family and had been raised in several different foster homes almost all her life after her mother died when she was just entering her teenage years and had also been abused as a teenager. Said he had taken advantage of her after meeting her and dating her for a short while because she did what she was told, but didn't know she was so very stupid to have left the baby unattended. Her father had long ago left her mother and her when she was very young and now suspected why he had. She would have to serve him like he wanted in order to make him happy or she could just fucking leave, and he didn't care if she had to live on the streets. Harold ended his brief hate filled speech before it jumped to a clip where the camera was focused into a room and the conversation was not very friendly at all as Betty sat crying as her husband stood in front of her and threatened her with a divorce, he said she was a stupid ass cunt and a worthless bitch and couldn't even keep their precious baby boy safe, and since she couldn't have any more children she was just a piece of useless human shit. The verbal abuse Harold subjected her too was tremendous and Carl noticed even during happier times her very submissive nature and wondered if this came from being raised in the foster care system and the abuse Harold had mentioned when she was younger and how he had taken advantage of her since the first day he met her. Harold had filmed most of the videos using a tri pod and this was evident from watching as he used the wide angle setting on the camera most of the time and only on occasions filmed her using the close up mode as he walked around filming her after subjecting her to his horrendous physical abuses. He began verbally humiliating her in the beginning and told her all she could do was clean the house and serve him like a good slave bitch as he grabbed her by her long hair and slapped her around several times before he began pulling out his belt and whipping her, making her kneel and lick his boots as he whipped her even more. This disc came to an end.

Carl now understood how it all had begun and fixed himself another good strong drink at the bar he had in his bedroom. He soon went and checked on Betty before returning to view more of the remaining video disc. He found her lying on her bed in the middle of the floor sleeping and closed the door behind him as he returned to his room and began viewing maybe the tenth or eleventh of thirty five or more discs, but first picked up the case with the laptop. He opened the case and found the charging cord and plugged it in and opened it up and turned it on, it booted up and it asked for a password, Carl looked in the carrying case and in a pocket found an index card, he looked and it contained the web and e-mail addresses and several different passwords, along with and some bondage and porn sites user names and passwords. After entering the password and the screen opened, there was the screen saver photo of Betty in her cage. Carl opened the documents and found just a few general generic files. But the photo and video files were massive, as he opened the photo file and it took over a minute to open all of the pictures in the file, they all were of Betty. Harold seemed to have kept and documented everything it seemed he had subjected her to. Carl closed that file and opened the video file and found it was divided into two files; one was labeled as being uploaded to an amateur B & D and S & M site, and that numbered twenty-eight videos covering several years. Carl viewed a couple as Betty was led around on a leash in a short video, then another as she was whipped as whelps and bruises were visible before she gave him oral sex. Carl turned the laptop off as he allowed the battery to charge up and it would take some time to investigate all it contained. He returned to viewing another disc as he popped the next one in, keeping them in sequence as he went along with his viewing and the scene was similar to the end of the last one, her husband Harold was berating his wife again, this was a different day, you could tell by their clothing and it was in a different room, but Harold said much the same things over and over again as Betty was now seriously beginning to show the effects of his sharp and very derogatory words, he told her he would divorce her and she would be homeless unless she did whatever he told her to do, because she was useless as a mother and since she could no longer conceive, said the only good thing she was good for was being a stupid whore. Betty was in tears and on the floor as he pulled her up by her hair again and slapped her several times and this time he spat in her face before he said she was going to serve him as a slave or he would put her out on the streets. She shook her head and begged him please no, several times before he told her to undress and lick his boots again as he removed his belt and told her to kneel and she complied, as he struck her buttocks with a thick wide leather belt. The next scene was a wide angle shot but with a few close ups as Betty was nude with a collar and leash on as Harold led her into the living room and bent her over after tying her hands behind her back and having her bend over a chair as he whipped her butt before he began having sex with her as she screamed and he now began to sodomized her. Carl viewed almost thirteen discs and watched as Harold increased his cruel savagery toward her. The things he did to her, as he watched, as she now began to rapidly lose weight over the following years. He had seen enough for one night and before he turned in walked through the house and made sure it was secure. He thought now about how Betty had been reduced down to the mentality of a slave, but understood the guilt she carried with her and couldn't or just wouldn't let it go. Harold kept her just healthy enough so he could continue to torment her and it had worked for a very, very long time and it probably came as a real sudden surprise as he took his last breath after hitting that tree.

Carl checked on Betty again, she was curled up in the center of the small bedroom sleeping and he wanted to just hold her and tell her everything would be all right, and decided not to until she started to move but she didn't wake up and decided to just leave her, closing the door behind him again. He went back to his room and since it was close to ten pm, decided to look at a few more disc since he was intrigued by what he was looking at and began to fast forward his viewing and stopping periodically to spot check through several of them since they were of Betty being whipped and humiliated, they were the gradual progression of Betty as a slave as he stopped at one where she was hanging from the ceiling and Harold was really pissed off now because he had been laid off from work and they were about to lose their house, her toes were just barely touching the floor and it appeared to be in a basement since the floor and walls were just bare concrete and she was completely naked as he inserted a large butt plug up into her now thinning body and had clothes pins on her nipples and her breast were tied with a large and very rough twine rope as they turned dark colors with several large industrial clamps on her swollen vagina lips and they looked like car battery jumper cable clamps, he stood back after spitting in her face, and began whipping her all over for a long time until she just hung there limp after blacking out. Soon after she had blacked out, he then returned with a bucket of ice cold water and threw it on her, reviving her before he started removing the clothes pins and clamps, anal plug and untying her breast and lowered her just slightly so her feet were flat on the floor but she was still stretched out, then he left her there as he turned out the lights. The videos were time stamped, and it picks up the next morning when he releases her now limp body and just lets her fall down onto the hard floor where she lays in her own excrement and urine that was now on the basement floor. And as she lays there he urinates on her then leaves the room before he returns several hours later and makes a very weak and humiliated Betty clean up her waste. The next scene was of her cleaning it up with her bare hands and placing it in a bucket as she was forced to then scrub the floor clean as he whipped her and then the video soon ends. The next is of her as she is stretched out on a plastic sheet on a bed, her limbs are tied to the four corners of a bed as Harold whips her vagina until its starts to swell, then he uses a vaginal pump as he pumps her and continues for several hours and half the time she is unconscious, as the video is turned on every hour for five minutes for about twelve hours before he finishes with her and makes her crawl around. It soon picks up two days later as she is hanging and he takes close ups and sits and says he had just joined an internet bondage site and was posting pictures of his slave slut wife on line for the whole world to see just how you treat a stupid cunt whore.

Carl recognized this web site as one he visited since he was voyeur of sorts. Harold now ties her breast and pumps her nipples in plastic tubes and when they come out the end of the short tubes ties them as they are stretched and now her permanently swollen vagina as he pumps her clitoris the same way and says he is going to make a freak bitch out of her. Harold gives the internet site kudos and says it's the best thing that has ever happened for him as he displays Betty without a care in the world as her face is seen on the World Wide Web. Carl looked and soon they had moved from the house and to the apartment she was living in now. Harold led her around with the collar and leash on as she complies to his every command as he orders her around, her body was thinning even more now as Carl scanned through the disc and stopped only when it appeared to be something new or the location changed and when he wanted to hear Harold's dialog. Harold now had the large animal cage he kept her in and the dog food bowls he fed her out of now.

Harold had sex with her whenever he wanted and would then lock her away in the cage and leave home as one disc showed when he left and then returned twenty-four hours later. Then there was the small mattress where she slept on the floor next to the bed where he chained her to the bed post. There were more scenes of him slapping her and making her beg for the meager and small amounts of food he would place in the doggie bowls as she was forced to eat and act like an animal if she wanted to be feed as he just sat back and laughed and when he was drunk had her anyway he wanted and sometimes inserted beer bottles inside of her, and in one he inserted a wine bottle with a long neck in her vagina and the whole time she offered no resistance, even when he had her arms clamped to her ankles and after having sex with her shook up a bottle of cheap Champaign and inserted it inside her vagina as she screamed and he laughed, and afterwards she would just say thank you master, or yes sir master, and please master. He had taken her outside wearing only a t-shirt, an a collar as he led her around on a dogs leash and when she asked to use the washroom, he made her squat as he made derogatory comments about his bitch ass dog wife. There was even one scene where he must have taken her to a park or forest preserve and led her around outside as he stripped her, then tied her to a tree and whipped her with his belt as she cried and when he untied her placed the leash back on her collar laughing as she began urinating. She was still nude when some hikers passed as he made her crawl like a dog and told them he was walking his bitch ass dog wife, they laughed and before they continued on their way Harold asked if they wanted to piss on the slut because she needed a drink, two of them did before they continued on their way. Betty was now being totally humiliated and degraded and after being exposed in public, and especially to other people now, she seemed to lose any resistance to whatever he subjected her to after that episode. Harold exposed her now more outside as he allowed in one video another man to whip her as she hung from a tree branch and when he cut her down they together urinated on her. Then the one where she was chained on the porch at the apartment as he grilled some meats, which he threw down some small pieces as she was made to eat them off the floor like an animal with only her mouth and Carl noticed after that her complete and utter surrender afterwards. Carl had seen more than enough for one day and decided to go to bed. He was tired and wondered how this would all now work out for him now.

Carl slept very well and after waking up and performing his usual morning routine before he went to check on his new house guest, Betty. She was awake and sitting on the floor on her mattress with her knees up in her chest, her thin arms wrapped around them with her head down. She looked up when he entered and he asked her how well did she sleep. Said she slept very well as he told her to stand up which she did and said for her to undress as she quickly removed the dress she had worn ever since yesterday and Carl said he wanted her to wash all of her clothes and to bath or shower every day and asked her if she understood. She replied yes sir, Master Carl as he showed her to the bathroom before bringing her a couple of bath towels and wash cloths and a bar of soap and some shampoo. He asked her to shower, and while she was bathing he brought back an extra-long t-shirt for her to wear. Asked her when she finished bathing to come downstairs without any shoes on. Carl felt sorry for her being probably very scared even now and stupid for not just leaving the abusive Harold. But he also understood the fear and the insecurity she must have felt, probably all her life and the harm it had but knew

66

that's what Harold had played on and had taken advantage of and why he was able to do the very cruel things he did to her over the years and it was now a permanent fixture in her mind. The best thing he felt he could do for her was to just leave her alone, letting her clean his house and treat her more like a normal person that needed some serious compassion and love and just maybe she would slowly come back around. But then again her submissive mentality probably started way before her marriage. But anyway he would be nice to her, it was his way and the only way he knew to treat someone and had never spanked or struck anyone since combat training in the army and especially a helpless woman or any woman.

Carl went downstairs and began fixing breakfast and brewed some coffee and made enough for him and now Betty. He had just finished cooking when she came downstairs with the clean shirt on and bare foot as instructed. He told her to sit as he placed a plate of eggs and bacon with a slice of toast before her and set his plate on the counter before coming around to sit next to her. Betty spoke and said thank you master Carl, and they ate in silence, then he asked her if she wanted any coffee, she said yes please master. Carl told her where the cups were as she rose and went and poured herself a cup before returning to finish eating. After they finished eating, Carl began to wash the dishes and then when Betty finished eating, she said please master, she would do it. She came over to the sink and began washing the dishes and placed them in the dish rack to dry as Carl sat and had another cup of coffee as he just looked at and watched her. When she finished Carl told her to bring all her clothes downstairs to the laundry room where he would be waiting. She departed and soon returned with all she owned as Carl showed her how to operate the washing machine. As he loaded her clothes into the machine, he noticed how worn out they really were. Said we have to get you some new clothes. He started the machine and then went upstairs to dress and had Betty follow him as he led her into his bedroom and she looked around and was surprised at how nice it was. He found some of his old shorts and told her to put them on, they were just a little too large for her and took them back and took out a pair of his athletic shorts he wore around the house with an elastic waistband and a draw string which worked out much better for her thin body. He told her to take the shirt off as he handed her one of his older t-shirts, one which was really too small for him but fit her so much better. Carl retrieved his cell phone and called the office and told them to call if they had any issues, said he had something important to do today and wouldn't be in. After he hung up, he told Betty to comb her hair and tie it up if she wanted to and bring her flat shoes downstairs. He began dressing and headed downstairs where he waited for Betty.

After she came downstairs they went to the garage and got in the car together and Carl headed for the Jacks Big Box Super Mart store to get Betty a few new clothes to start her new life with. He didn't have to ask her age, he knew once he had went through all her documents, she was now thirty seven, five foot eight inches tall and he was going to treat her like a real person as they pulled up to the entrance, and then exited the car. Carl had her walk in front of him and she was very sexy with the shorts on as he looked at her slender shape. They went to the women's section after he had gotten a shopping cart and Carl filled it with a variety of clothing items that would fit her now and knew she would gain some weight once she began eating better and on a more regular schedule, more like every day so he only picked out no more than three or four of any one item. He had her try on some athletic shoes and made sure they fit, picked a pair of low heeled dress shoes and even bought her some cosmetics like lip stick and nail polish before they checked out. He then headed to the Sexy store that had costumes and stockings, panty hose and toys, and even vibrators that you could control with a cell phone; he purchased a couple pairs of stockings and a body suit along with a maid's costume. When he finished shopping they headed back home and had Betty carry the clothing to her bedroom, the one she was sleeping in and told her to place all her clothing in the closet, it had modular shelving, so she would have no problems keeping it neat. Carl handed her the maids costume and told her to put it on. He stood and watched as she undressed and dressed, when she finished he told her to put on the hi-heel shoes and he had her stand by a bare wall and took several pictures of her. He then told her to undress and put the shorts and t- shirt back on and come downstairs as he quickly left her bedroom. Carl was turned on seeing her naked and since he hadn't been with a woman in a very long time was doing all he could to suppress his sexual feelings, but Betty would be safe here with him because he had no intentions of having a relationship with her, since he truly felt sorry for her. When Betty came downstairs Carl showed her where the cleaning supplies were located and instructed her to wear the surgical gloves to protect her hands and told her he would get her some work smocks and showed and told her what he wanted done and everything kept neat and clean and said in a few days they would donate her husband's clothes to charity and have all her business squared away. She said thank you Master Carl.

She asked him, master what do you want me to do now? And Carl took her downstairs to the enormous basement and asked her to mop the tile floor, and showed her a mop and bucket and the wash basin in a wet closet with supplies. He also told her all the bathrooms were to be cleaned each and every day regardless of being used or not and he would be checking to be sure they were all done properly. Betty began filling the bucket with water and soap. The bucket had a wringer and soon she was hard at work mopping as Carl left and took out some chicken breast for dinner. Carl decided to keep a written record of her weight and a photo record as well. Carl went to his bedroom and turned on his computer at his desk that was located near the balcony window and brought up the home cameras that were located throughout the house and pulled up the basement camera and watched as Betty began mopping the large floor. He then decided to pick up where he left off looking at the video record her husband Harold had made. He checked the next one in sequence and now Betty was on her back, hands tied to her ankles with a broom handle keeping her legs spread open, as Harold berated her and applied a large bottle of cooking oil to her as he poured it on her and used a funnel to fill her anal cavity as he laughed and had a very large dildo that he slowly inserted into her anus as she screamed, he worked it back and forth slowly until the massive object was halfway inside of her and soon Betty stopped screaming and began to seemingly enjoy it before Harold pulled it out slowly and then took a very slim metal baseball bat that he greased up and began inserting into her, after a while he just let it stay in her as he began placing clothes pins on her now enlarged vaginal lips as Betty moaned in displeasure and begged him to please stop as he took pictures with the SLR camera and ignored her frantic pleas which he of course ignored. He eventually removed the bat and clothes pins and then removed the broom handle and untied her and bent her over and then sodomized her. The next clip was Betty hanging spread eagle upside down as Harold cruelly whipped her enlarged vagina even more until it was so very swollen and red it looked like a huge red beet between her thighs, she was gagged and crying as he then whipped her breast, it seemed over the passing of years he developed a real hatred for her as his punishments became so much more degrading and very cruel. When he finished, turn her right side up, still spread eagle as he used the large office type binder clips on her now very swollen vaginal lips as she screamed through the gag and then hung weights from them, when she blacked out he removed the clamps and revived her then placed her in the large animal cage as she cried profusely. Carl couldn't believe some of the things he had seen so far. He looked at several more and stopped as Harold tied her enlarged and very swollen vagina with a leather boot lace before he whipped her, as she screamed again until she fainted, then he just continued whipping her as she hung from the ceiling and just left her hanging as he photographed her for his bondage site uploads. Carl in fast forward mode spot checked and looked as he began pausing along the way to hear what was being said.

After nearly finishing the entire video album with about seven more disc left he looked as Harold had her on a large living room type chair with her hands tied above and behind her head, before he tied her legs with her ankles above and behind her head, leaving her now fully exposed, her shaven vagina area and anus fully exposed along with the back of her thighs, as he took a wide leather strap and whipped her vagina and thighs until it was very swollen and tender as evident by the now crimson color, again he knelt down and licked her now very large and very swollen and super sensitive clit and as she began to show signs of enjoyment, he laughs out loud as he looks into the camera with a very fiendish grin then applies some cooking oil to her before he then returns with large bottle of hot sauce and pours it completely out on her tender thighs, vagina and anus as she screams, a scream like nothing like Carl had ever heard before, as she cries and begs him for mercy and to please stop, and then with a rubber glove on he rubes her vagina and anus and plays with her as he inserts a finger inside both of her holes as she screamed before he stands back and laughs as he takes his SLR and takes several shots as she goes in and out of consciousness before he takes a powerful industrial type blower, similar to one you use to dry paint with and begins blowing off the hot sauce, then applying a large vibrator to her vagina and clitoris until she just totally blacked out unconscious. He now returns and pours ice cold water on her as she shivers and screams again and inserts an ice cube in her vagina and this time blacks completely out. He attempts to get her conscious with no response as he releases her legs but leaves her tied to the post. Twenty minutes pass before she shows any signs of consciousness. After releasing her he makes her bathe in the bath tub as she cries the entire time before he makes her oil her body then locks her in the cage naked and then leaves. Carl had to have a drink after that one. When Carl resumes, and continued where he left off, it seems that Harold resorted to hanging weights from her nipples after pumping them into the small narrow clear plastic tubes as they are now stretched several inches inside the tube, removing the pump and then tying the end of her nipple so they would stay in the tube, this explained why they were now over an inch long. He also pumped her vagina with a pump sometimes after he whipped her vagina and it begins to swell and has almost remained that way even now. Then using the binder clips on her very swollen vaginal lips and those clothes hangers with clamps on her breast as he clamped her nipples and taking numerus pictures, and even placed the clamps several times on her swollen clitoris. He even sucked her clit up into the narrow tubes one a little larger than the ones he used on her nipples also while she was tied up and helpless. But the most cruel one was him taking a blow torch when he rubbed her vaginal area as he had her legs spread wide open and you could see the short hairs on her vagina and used the torch on her as the hairs burned and she screamed until she again blacked out as he continued and didn't stop, then another where he placed duct tape on her mouth, nipples and vagina. Another time after pumping her vagina and it was truly swollen had a piece of duct tape with thumb tacks attached as he taped it to her very tightly before making her walk around as tears flowed from her eyes and he laughed and continued whipping her. But the strange thing was in the last six videos when Harold begins to talk about the end being near and makes reference it will be ten years since the birth of Ronald and was planning to have a celebration by taking out the trash and burying or burning it and it could also be financially beneficial to him. By the time Carl had finished looking at all the video disc he was in tears and crying, holding his head in his hands. It took him a while before he was able to compose himself. He could never have imagined doing what he had just seen to anyone, ever, it was pure outright torture. After another drink and getting himself emotionally together he turned on the home camera and watched as Betty continued to mop the basement floor, she was more than half way finished as Carl looked at her and began crying all over again and wondered about how much more abuse she had endured over the years that wasn't recorded or photographed. But what bothered him the most was what Harold meant near the end that was of real concern, when he said the end was near and it was time to dispose of the shit in his life.

An hour later Carl had found the web site Harold had used and brought up the pictures he had posted after he joined in order to have access which was free thank god as he viewed and saw Betty as she was exposed to the world and there were more than pictures, there also were videos and it numbered close to a six hundred photos Harold had uploaded over the past few years and the last ones were just a week before his untimely death. After he had smoked a joint and had another stiff drink Carl was able to go downstairs and check on Betty, she was finishing up and Carl was going to keep a record of her starting today. When she finished Carl had taken his digital camera out, made sure the date was correct and told her she had done a very good job. Then he instructed her to undress and stand by a wall that was dark green in color, to stand up straight as he took pictures of her front, back, and both sides and then close ups of her face, vagina and rectum before having her go to the bathroom and stand on a scale and took a picture of the digital readout, and checked that it showed in the camera, she weighed one hundred ten and a half pounds. When he finished he told her to dress. He told her to come and stand in front of him which she did, he looked her in her eyes and reached out and hugged and held her tight. Carl held her and she hugged him back and they both began to cry. Carl held her a long time and rubbed her back and explained he wasn't going to abuse her, whip or punish her in any way ever and that she was safe here then asked her if she understood, she looked up at him and said yes sir master Carl. He asked if she would help him prepare dinner. She said yes sir master Carl. Betty was a great help as Carl had her peel the potatoes and carrots for dinner as he seasoned and prepared to bake the chicken for dinner. He sat her down and asked her what she wanted to do, and all she would ever say was that she was here to serve him. When the food had finished cooking, Carl dished them up and they sat in the booth and ate together as Carl found himself just looking at her as he wondered why she was here now and in his life. She looked up at him and smiled at him, it was the first time she had done so in a very, very long time.

# Four

After several days, almost a week had passed, Carl took some time off from his busy schedule and stopped at a local furniture store that sold quality merchandise and purchased a bedroom set, which consisted of a queen sized platform bed, with side tables and a dresser. He also purchased a large couch with a matching chair and also a fifty-five inch wall mounted television for Betty's bedroom. He made sure he was at home when it was all delivered and had it placed and the television installed in her bedroom. Then he took her roll up mattress, pillow and blanket and threw them all away along with her flat worn out shoes. He also bought four sets of sheets and a couple of pillows and two blanket sets for her bed. He told Betty she was to sleep in the bed and not on the floor any longer. Since it was still early in the day Carl told Betty to dress and he told her to wear one of her new dresses and look presentable. He took her to the garage as he informed her they were going to the bank and Carl brought along all her banking records and took her to the bank so she could open a new checking account and close her and Harold's old ones, transferring the monies into a new checking account and the pass book with the 26 thousand dollars into a certificate of deposit. After entering and signing in, they were soon shown to a booth at the bank. The bank representative proceeded to process the request Carl had made and informed him of what business Mrs. Betty Johnson needed taken care of. The banker asked Betty who was going to be the second on the account with her; she didn't hesitate to say Carl was to be on all her accounts. After finishing the bank business they went to her old apartment and arrived several minutes before the donation people. Carl had made arrangements with them to take the furniture away as he and Betty checked the apartment again for any papers they may have overlooked the weeks prior when Carl had taken her home with him. Carl folded up the large animal cage and placed it in the trunk of his car before returning upstairs where Betty waited and couldn't explain why he had decided to take it. Soon the apartment was empty and together they proceeded to clean up and remove any trash, and food that was left as they disposed of in the trash dumpster outside. Carl had her write a check for the remaining one months' rent and then they went to the apartment office to inform them the unit was empty and to schedule an inspection so she could get her security deposit back before the lease ran out. It wasn't very long before the two insurance companies for the life insurance policies on Harold had contacted Carl. He informed them of Betty's new checking account information and they soon made electronic deposits of the insurance moneys after they had received by mail the certified copies of the death certificates. Carl then took her a couple days later, to the social security office and she received the burial benefits and also would start receiving a monthly check based on Harold's earnings which they arraigned to go automatically into her new checking account and it was about a grand a month. After the insurance was deposited he again took her back to the bank and had her place the majority of the insurance money in long term certificates of deposits for the maximum interest rates if it remained untouched for three years. Carl soon found out that Harold had a pension plan that paid Betty a monthly amount of close to twelve hundred dollars a month as a beneficiary and her medical coverage was automatically deducted from it so she was still covered, and all of this had been set up before he started to subjecting Betty to his abuse and he had never changed anything after they were married which turned out to be very fortunate for her. He must have loved her very much at one time, or just didn't bother to change anything since there weren't any other relatives to leave anything to. Carl had arraigned for that monthly check to be deposited into her checking account as well. She had a valid driver's license and Carl took her to the DMV for a change of address. Now all her documents were up to date. She wasn't a poor woman by any means; she had just been subject to abuse mentally and also physically, and now Carl felt better because he had kept her from being further abused by anyone else who would have definitely taken advantage of her based on her fragile state of mind.

Other than cleaning the house, Carl really didn't have very much or anything for Betty to do besides wash and clean the large almost empty house and wash his clothes and decided she should iron all his clothes and sheets just to keep her busy. He had her clean everything daily, even the empty bedrooms and just made sure she slept in her bed. He let her cook sometimes but he did most of the cooking and there was always something for her to eat and made sure she did along with taking her vitamins. One Saturday morning since Carl was slowly decorating his new home with its hard wood floors, he had a large area rug along with a sofa set and a couple of large comfortable chairs along with a wide cabinet and television delivered a few weeks before and placed in the living room, around the same time he had purchased Bettys bedroom set. He was sitting after having had breakfast with Betty a couple hours earlier on the new living room couch looking at and programing the new television since he hadn't had time since its delivery when Betty soon approached after cleaning up the kitchen after breakfast and several other rooms as she did every day. Betty knelt down directly in front of him, and asked if the master was happy with her. Carl said he was very satisfied with her work around the house. It had now been slightly more than eight weeks or so since bringing Betty here. She asked him if he loved her. He said that she was very special to him and cared for her very much. Then asked her why she was asking him these particular questions. She told him he had treated her very well but hadn't punished, whipped or even spanked her since the very first day and wondered also why he hadn't had sex with her and said she knew he was aroused when he looked at her. Carl only had her undress before him once a week as he kept track of her physical appearance and body weight and hadn't used her in any sexual way what's so ever, abused or exposed her in any way like Harold had.

Carl looked at her and asked her if she was happy being here, to which she replied she was very happy and felt he cared about her very much but didn't know if he loved her because he hadn't punished her or spoken to her harshly or in a derogatory manor. She told Carl that a good master must punish his slaves to show them he loved them. Carl looked at her and felt pity for her thinking this way and said he did love her and didn't need to abuse or demean her to show his love for her. He asked her what she thought he should do to her. She replied that he needed to whip her to show her his true love and then take and use her anyway he wanted. Carl said that wasn't necessary and that she had it all wrong, that love wasn't meant to be painful, humiliating or degrading. Then she began begging him and started crying, saying please Master Carl, please use me. He told her when he was ready to punish her she would know. She looked up at him and begged him to please punish her now, over and over again. Carl began getting upset as she began making demands and told her a slave makes no demands on her master and if she continued her punishment would be even more severe, and ordered her to go to her bedroom. She now acted very reluctantly and hesitated on purpose, just like a disobedient child. Carl noticed her insubordination, and then ordered her to the basement. There were hooks in the ceiling in the basement in various locations and he decided he would strip her naked and hang her up before deciding what he would do to her. It wasn't something Carl was looking forward to doing since he had seen the way Harold had abused her, but she really wanted to be used and abused. It was less than an hour before noon on a very pleasant Saturday morning when this particular and very first incident occurred since bringing Betty here to his home. Carl went upstairs to his closet and brought down the suitcase with all the bondage equipment he had taken from the apartment that Harold had used on his wife. Carl hadn't touched the suit case since placing the many items in it when he moved her here. Carl thought this was going to be the first time since being with him he would have to punish her, not because he wanted to, but because she insisted. Carl had hoped she would get over that phase of what had happened in her past life but evidently not, and now he would have to do to her what she wanted. He also realized that deep down inside he was also turned on and was enjoying her submission to him as it played into that dark, hidden and very repressed part of his ego where he always thought about doing something close to what was about to occur and had masturbated and gotten off on many times in the past. When he reached the basement Betty was standing near the stairs just as he had ordered. He told her to undress; she was slowly gaining her weight back and looking much less gaunt and actually had gained about close to eight pounds since being here and since weighing her the last time. Carl placed the suitcase on the bar and removed a pair of wrist cuffs, then the neck collar and placed them on her. He found a couple lengths of chain about four feet long that turned out to be just long enough to reach from the ceiling hooks to her wrist cuffs. He attached them to her wrist and found the ceiling hooks were spaced about four feet apart. Since the ceiling was high for a basement as he attached one to each arm, she was spread out perfectly, with only a few links left in the chains as he used almost the entire length. Betty's arms were now stretched out as he looked into her pretty face and said to her; he didn't want to hurt her and really felt this was truly unnecessary and had hoped she would be relieved that her torment had ended. She looked at him and said please master Carl, please use me, I need this to function now, please whip me, hurt me as tears came to her pretty brown eyes, and she continued to beg him to use her as she cried. He then went and found a blind fold and before placing it on her, he stood looking into her eyes, and said she was forcing him to do this to her and said he had hoped she would have gotten over being abused physically. He told her it wasn't her place to make demands on him and he didn't believe in beating women, but because she had been insolent and very disrespectful she would hang here until he decided just what punishment he felt was necessary for her to become more obedient, and asked her if she understood what he just said, she replied yes sir master Carl. He kissed and held her and said he loved her very much as she then began crying. He placed the blindfold on her, and detected a strange sense of happiness in her response as she now smiled back at him and said thank you as Carl now realized she had just forced his hand into doing what he never thought he would ever do. He thought if he just let her hang here and did nothing, what would she do next, what might her response be a rebellion of sorts from her dissatisfaction, should he risk it, or just follow through and punish her as he satisfied her and now his own dark side. Carl decided to make her happy and also satisfy his own inner demons, this being a completely new experience for him.

Carl left her hanging as he looked at her, and began admiring her nude body, her breast were starting to regain their firmness as were her hips and butt also, her vagina was plump from all the years of being beaten and pumped as her now large clit stuck out like a little penis waiting to come out of hiding. As she hung there Carl went and began caressing and feeling her body. He closely watched her response and enjoyed feeling and touching her soft skin as she responded to his soft and sensual touch as she was now becoming very highly aroused as he caressed her calf's, thighs, stomach, breast as his fingers gently roamed over her touching her vagina and around to her buttocks, as he bit her neck, licked her ear as a shiver now went through her. He decided to place the vibrator he had just purchased that you could control from a cell phone inside her vagina only after he slowly and sensually worked a large and long anal plug into her welcoming rectum after finding it in the suitcase and applying liberal amounts of lubricant to her anus that he also found inside the suitcase. He then took a piece of rope and looped it around her waist in front of her, then between her legs holding the vibrator in place making sure her extra-large clitoris was between the two large ropes, and then tying it tightly in the back as it held the anal plug in place as it passed tightly between both of her round butt cheeks. He placed the ankle cuffs on her and hooked them both together, before tying a short length of rope he also found around her knees. Carl stepped back and looked at her and took some pictures with his cell phone before he departed leaving her to hang there as he looked at the clock and it was a few minutes now after noon as he returned to the living room and turned off the television before deciding to make himself a sandwich and have a bowl of soup. He was in no particular hurry since it was Saturday his day off and had nothing else to do as he sat down and ate his sandwich and soup and took his time. He waited and for little over an hour before returning to the basement and sat at the bar and had his phone with him and brought up the app for the vibrator. Betty had been just hanging with nothing happening as Carl figured she was having thoughts about what was going to happen next. Carl looked at the app controller now as he activated the device. It had several different modes and you could also vary the intensity as Carl started with the lowest setting, as he watched Betty hanging as she began reacting to the vibrations that now coursed through her most sensitive parts as he fixed himself a drink and then returned to the other side of the bar and just sat and watched her as she slowly began to shake and moan now with some minor spasms that would soon bring her to a very intense and continuing organism. Then he turned it to pulse, her large clit was between the ropes he had tied tightly between her thin firm thighs and watched as it was starting now to protrude and emerge from its protective covering, looking like a head with a hood on, she was starting to twist slightly as he turned it to a constant setting and very slowly turned the intensity up and her moans became louder as her breathing quickened. He knew she could take it and much more especially after what Harold had subjected her to in the past; he wasn't hurting her, but giving her very intense pleasure, something new for her to experience as he had observed Harold never allowed her to really pleasure herself as she only had organisms after being severely punished on her vagina and nipples. She started to sweat, dance around and moan even more loudly, it was a beautiful sight to behold. Then his doorbell rang and he turned the vibrator down to a lower setting but left it on. He left as he ascended the stairs to see who was at his front door.

After reaching the front door and looking out through the peep hole, observed it was his nearest neighbor from directly across the street, Mr. Timothy Rogers as he opened the front door and warmly greeted him and welcomed him inside. Tim Rogers stepped inside and said he hoped everything was going well for him. Carl said it was as Tim began to explain his reason for being here and wanted to know if he would be so kind as to attend a small gathering they, his wife and him were going to have the following day. Carl said sure he would be very delighted and would love to attend, and then asked Tim if he wanted him to bring anything. Tim said no, but if he wanted to he could and stated he really hoped Carl would attend because there would be quite a few single women there, friends of his wife and he really needed some single unattached bachelors to attend. Tim Rogers stated his wife had insisted that he should be invited because he was single and available and also because some of her many girlfriends were single. Tim said they had been married just over a year and this was kind of an informal anniversary celebration of sorts and said it was also a very casual affair and would be outside as well. Carl asked him at about what time should he make an appearance, and Tim said around two or three o'clock would be just perfect. Carl thanked him as he and Tim Rogers again shook hands before he turned to depart and walk back down his driveway as Carl closed his front door. Well he thought what a surprise and felt he was going to have some fun.

When Carl returned to the basement where Betty was hanging, found she had urinated as it ran down her thigh as she pissed again when he returned as she was having continuous orgasms now and breathing hard and moaning as Carl turned the vibrator up for five or six more minutes before turning it slowly down and then off. He took one of the several different whips out of the suit case, and decided Betty now needed a good whipping. She was standing in her own piss bare foot as Carl began whipping her lightly at first; he started with her backside which was a real surprise for her as she jerked in response to the whip that was now caressing and wrapping around her soft smooth body as he began with her ass, thighs, and back before he whipped her in in front on her breast, stomach and thighs. Then he went back and decided on using the vibrator again, this time he gradually turned it up to the max as she began to moan and then just began screaming. Carl began whipping her again all over. She was now having multiple climaxes and soon she just hung there limp. He turned the vibrator off and let her hang there as he removed the mop and bucket from the closet and mopped up the urine from the floor. Then he removed the blindfold and found Betty had completely passed out. He went to the bar and filled an ice bucket with very cold water, returned and poured it over her as she slowly came back around. He looked at her and held her face with one hand, and slapped her several times on both sides of her face, she was conscious as he spoke to her and addressed her as his slave bitch and asked her if she had enough. She spoke softly and said she was here to serve her new master. Carl found himself getting caught up in what he detested as he spat in her face and rubbed it across her pretty face and said to her she was a piece of shit and asked her if she wanted more. And to his complete and utter surprise she said, yes sir please Master Carl, whip me more please. He mopped up the water and pushed the bucket aside and returned to the bar, picked up his phone and turned the vibrator on again and found another leather whip that was more cruel looking and used it on her a couple of times before he stopped and turned the vibrator off and began to untie her knees and unhooked her ankles, but left the vibrator and butt plug in with the rope between her legs. Carl used the same length of rope and attached it to one of the ankle cuffs and pulled her left leg up behind her as he reached up and attached it to the hook in the ceiling, causing Betty to stand on one leg and her crotch to become fully exposed. Carl had seen this in some of the Oriental bondage videos and magazines as he now had a significant hard on. He returned to the suit case and found the office binder clips that were used to secure several dozen pieces of paper and applied them to her now protruding nipples as she winced in pain. Betty was now entering the zone where as he looked into her face and asked her if she was satisfied now. And her reply was yes sir Master Carl, as she begged him to please hurt her even more. Carl stepped back and looked at her, before returning and releasing the rope from between her legs, removing the clamps from her nipples and attaching them to her vaginal lips. He pulled her swollen nipples as she jerked from his touch. He then returned to the bar and turned the remote vibrator on again as Betty jerked violently on one leg as he varied the sensations before he turned it off completely after about ten minutes, and walking over and pulling it out of her. He removed the clamps from her now very swollen vaginal lips and rubbed her between her legs as he told her she was his slut bitch and she had better obey or worse would happen to her. Just then she erupted with a massive climax as he then began fingering her now swollen vagina and pinched her protruding and sensitive clitoris. Carl untied the rope holding her ankle behind her and eased her leg down until she was standing on two feet. He then released her arms and had to catch her as he laid her limp body down on the cool tile floor and looked down at her as he now stepped behind the bar and dropping his shorts and taking his penis in his hand and very quickly jerked off, as a massive amount of hot sperm shot quickly out filling his hand. Carl sat a few minutes breathing hard as he used a paper towel to wipe his hands as he looked at Betty sprawled out on the basement floor now fully satisfied and himself also.

He let her lie there for a long time close to an hour until she was able to move and then made her kneel before him as he took and hooked the leash to her collar and made her crawl around the large basement as he whipped her as she slowly crawled. Soon he stopped and made her stand. He found a vibrating dildo in the suitcase and stuck it in her mouth and ordered her to lick it with her tongue. He turned her around and cuffed her hands behind her, before turning her back around to face him and stuck the dildo against her now very swollen and enlarged clitoris working the dildo between her thighs as she jerked with another massive climax as he held the leash making her stand. He turned her around and bent her over as he removed the butt plug from her ass and placed it on a paper towel after wiping it off. He pulled the leash again making her stand and face him as he asked her again if she had enough, to which she replied she was here to serve her master. Carl made her crawl to the cage he had brought from her apartment and placed her in it, locking it as he started cleaning up the basement floor, dildos and anal plug and placing them all back inside the suit case. When he finished he looked at Betty in her cage and she seemed to be very, very happy now. Carl thought how fucked up she really was, but now she was his responsibility and thought about how he should have kept his mouth shut that fateful day in the supermarket. After cleaning up Carl departed and prepared dinner and fixed some spaghetti sauce from scratch and cleaned up as he left the sauce in the pan. After he finished cooking about an hour later in the late afternoon Carl went downstairs and opened the cage and released Betty, making her stand as he removed the collar and cuffs and lead her to the center of the floor, he told her to stand with her arms behind her back, legs spread and told her he was going to exhibit her to his neighbors and have her serve them also. He asked her what she thought of that, and said whatever the master wanted. He asked her if she thought he loved her now, to which she replied, oh yes sir, Master Carl.

He said, she would have her serve his guess in the nude with just her collar on and she would be commanded to serve everyone and do whatever they wanted and asked her if she was going to obey him. She responded and said she was here to serve her master and she was his property to do whatever he wished of her. He told her to stand there and only speak if she had to use the bathroom, she said, yes sir, Master Carl.

Carl fixed himself another drink, sat and just looked at her, she was very pretty and looking better with every passing day since she had been eating better and on a regular basis and besides he had also been giving her vitamins. She was starting to show a marked improvement in her overall appearance as her breast began to regain some of their former shape and size along with her buttocks, thighs and legs and figured soon she would be looking so much better. He thought how Harold had really fucked up her mind and taken undue advantage of her and hoped that would soon change one day like her body was showing improvements. He also wondered how so many men would love having such an obedient female as a slave, or the so called perfect wife. After making her stand there almost an hour he told Betty to go shower and clean herself up and to oil her skin, and then come downstairs and help him prepare dinner. When she did he had long since finished cooking much earlier even before he sent her upstairs and had her set the table as he prepared their plates. She ate and said she loved his food very much. She asked Carl was he really going to exhibit her like he said. He looked at her and asked her why was she was asking him questions again. Said she was his slave and didn't want to serve anyone but him, and said please Master Carl; she only wanted to serve him. He said you will serve as a maid if I have a party and you will wait on the guess. He asked her if that was acceptable to her, she said yes sir master Carl. She asked if he would have sex with her, to which he said he would think about it. She said please Master Carl, she would please him anyway he wanted. He said he would think about it and would soon let her know.

He told Betty to clean up and he would come back and check when she finished, he returned, checked and found she had done an excellent job and everything was in order. And since he was pleased he ordered her to follow him as he led her to his bedroom and told her to undress. He had her stand before him as he undressed and asked her how did she want to please her master. He was sitting on the couch and she came over and knelt down and Carl could see the whelps and whip marks from earlier in the day still visible on her body, she bent down and took him in her hands and placed him in her mouth and soon he was very hard and she sucked and licked him and very soon he climaxed in her mouth and filled it completely as Betty swallowed all he had to give and none spilled from her hungry and eager to please mouth, Carl pulled her head up as she licked her lips and told her to kneel in the bed, she did as he rubbed her marked ass and looked at her closely as he felt her between her legs, he told her to lay on her back and to hold her ankles, causing her to be exposed to his gaze, he had some oil and returned as she held herself open and he applied the oil to her, feeling her warm vagina and watching as she responded to his touch, he played with her vaginal lips and as she became more aroused and her clit started to protrude, he massaged her as she soon exploded unexpectedly, panting as he played with her as he rubbed her anus as it was beckoning for attention. She lay panting as her pussy dripped with moisture as Carl placed three fingers inside of her and then remembered how Harold had inserted a baseball bat into her anus. He soon had his three fingers inside her vagina and used his thumb on her clit, causing her to have another explosive climax and soon he had his hand inside of her as she was going wild and continued to climax until she just collapsed and he removed his hand. Carl then played with her anus and soon it opened up as she grabbed his hand and forced it deeper inside of her, she was ecstatic as Carl played with and pinched her clit with his other hand as she had an even more intense climax than before. Carl withdrew his hand from her ass as she just lay there, breathing hard and left to wash his hands. When he returned Carl ordered her up and to her bedroom. She looked at Carl and asked if she had pleased him, he said yes for now. He asked her if she was now satisfied and she said, yes sir master Carl and he had made her very, very happy, but was sorry he didn't take her. Carl told her maybe later.

Carl ordered her to her bedroom and told her to shower, douche, and then oil herself before going to bed and he would check to be sure she followed his instructions. She said yes sir master Carl and departed. Carl thought what Harold had done to her was almost irreversible. After about an hour later he entered her bedroom and inspected her to see if she had followed his instructions. Carl told her to get some sleep as she smiled and said she loved him very much.

# Five

Carl woke up to a beautiful sunny Sunday morning; the sky was clear and cloudless. It would be one beautiful Sunday and was the day of the casual get together across the street and you couldn't have picked a more pleasant day with the temperatures in the upper seventies and very low humidity and hardly any clouds in a beautiful blue sky. Carl had breakfast with Betty and she cleaned up afterwards as usual, and mentioned to her that he wanted the basement thoroughly cleaned after she had urinated on the floor yesterday and to be sure and use the pine cleaner along with bleach, and when she finished with the basement, to clean all the bathrooms in the entire house. Said he would check each one later and they should be clean enough for her to drink from the toilet. He asked her if she understood, she replied yes sir, Master Carl. Even though she cleaned the bathrooms daily Carl repeated himself so there would be no misunderstanding what so ever as Betty followed his instructions to the letter. He also told her if she finished before he returned to begin waxing all the wood floors, starting with downstairs. She said, yes sir, Master Carl. Carl returned to his bedroom after giving Betty her instructions for the day and began checking his computer. When he finished looking at his e-mails and other interesting items he checked the house cameras and watched as Betty began cleaning the basement, starting with the floor, he watched her for a short time before preparing himself for the get together across the street later on that evening. He took his time preparing since he had several hours and anyway it was a Sunday. Carl had a funny feeling something really special was about to happen today as he prepared to take a long an relaxing bath an afterwards a quick rinse in the shower before taking out a clean pair of dress shorts and a fancy t-shirt, oiling his body before he dressed and applying some natural bug repellent that had a very pleasant smell in place of a cologne. Carl went downstairs and fixed himself a sandwich and ate and took his daily regimen of vitamins before he would leave shortly. He returned to his bedroom and looked at the cameras and checked on Betty's progress before he departed, he had his phone and could checkup on her any time while he was gone. He went downstairs just as she was just finishing up with the basement floor and was just beginning to start on the bathrooms, starting with the one in the basement. She looked up at him and asked if he was satisfied. He walked around and checked and returned to where she was standing and told her so far it would pass. He told her to continue as he went upstairs and left some hidden marks in each bathroom just to see if she did as she was told before he departed.

Carl then went to his wine closet and picked out a couple bottles of some very good wines, some which he really enjoyed and placed inside a small canvas tote bag, as he chose one red and one white and soon departed as he walked down his long driveway and across the street. He was warmly greeted by Tim and Gloria Rogers. Gloria introduced him to the entire group of guests who were present. There weren't many married couples but a few unmarried and quite attached couples. Most of the women were her close and very single girlfriends. It was about three thirty in the evening when he first arrived and he was soon having a pretty good time as he soon meet several very interesting, and very pretty and highly intelligent single women, but it seems only one found him attractive enough to single him out. He had begun to strike up a conversation with his host when this one particularly really beautiful woman seemed to really show a keen interest in him as she made it a point of introducing herself to him a second time shortly after arriving and having been introduced to everyone present. She really appealed to him also, she was an exceptionally beautiful woman with a very exotic appearance with a light sepia completion, dark brunette and long wavy and thick hair, and had a very shapely figure, she stood about five foot six and was a year older than he after having a brief conversation as it slipped out in a quick conversation, she was single, and as they talked, found out they had quite a bit in common, her name was Sarah Anne Rogers, no relation to his host. Soon the conversation revolved around many different subjects and somehow touched on the subject of marriage briefly, she stated it almost happened to her once, but realized it just wasn't going to work out at that particular time and was very happy she didn't do it then as time passed and things really began looking up for her. She went on to say the unfortunate guy ended up going to jail for bank fraud. But then she said that didn't mean it wasn't something she wouldn't do, it would very much depend on the other person as well. After a short discussion about business, said she was a certified public accountant and owned her own accounting firm. She was highly intelligent and very soft spoken and Carl felt really attracted to her and really felt at ease in her presence, as they seemed to have quickly formed a serious mutual bond. Everyone gathered thought they might have known one another before today since they both seemed to only be interested in one another that evening. Their host came over and jokingly said they needed to break this up, they looked at her, and laughed since they had been so enthralled talking together they had completely ignored everyone else. When Sarah stepped inside briefly to use the bathroom, Carl pulled out his phone and checked on Betty. She was busy cleaning his bedroom bathroom upstairs, which was very good as he watched until she returned. When Sarah returned, she informed Carl that she would really like to go out with him some time, he was elated at this prospect and said that sounded fantastic and said it would be a real pleasure for him to be in the company of one as beautiful as she. They discussed the business they were in more and exchanged business cards and very much enjoyed each other's company. In their long and ongoing conversation Carl had made it clear he was a home body but didn't mind going out every now and then, but really enjoyed being at home and cooking, reading and just plain relaxing and enjoying his home. The evening seemed to pass very quickly and the next thing Carl knew he was walking Sarah to her car when she decided to leave because she had to work the following day. Carl then returned to the party and thanked his neighbor the Rogers for the invitation and said he really enjoyed himself and departed as he headed back home. When he returned Betty was just beginning to start waxing the floors and he let her continue with her work. He asked her if she had eaten, she said no that she had to finish her duties first. Carl went upstairs to change and checked that she had done what she was told and found she had as the hidden marks he had left were all gone before returning downstairs and fixing a pizza for the both of them. He told her when she finished the living room she could stop and finish the rest of the house tomorrow.

When the pizza was ready he told her to wash her hands and come eat. She sat down and Carl served her. She said thank you master as she devoured the pizza since she hadn't eaten since breakfast. It wasn't long before they finished and Carl complimented her on a job well done. She was very musty and sweaty as Carl told her to go shower and go to bed, she said yes sir master Carl and departed to put her wax and mop away before going to her bedroom. It was late evening and Carl went outside and sat on his deck with a drink before turning in and having a wonderful day. He had finally met someone he really seemed to like very much and decided he would date Ms. Sarah Anne Rogers.

A couple of weeks actually passed before Carl had his first date with Ms. Sarah Rogers, and that didn't occurred until they both had time away from there busy schedules and weren't tired. After several more months had passed and a few more evenings spent together on dates outside of home they began seeing each other on a fairly regular basis, maybe once every other week or so, they hadn't had sex yet, as they were just going out to dinner and the movies and truly enjoying one another's company and giving themselves a break from their everyday routines and developing a real steady and close friendship as they got to know how they felt about things in general and found they held the same opinions most of the time. He had told Sarah he had a house keeper when they were talking about their home life and Sarah thought that was very wonderful and invited her to dinner at his house one week day and Carl had cooked and had Betty clean up the house and made sure everything was to his satisfaction. He fed Betty before Sarah arrived and sent her to her bedroom where she stayed before and after Sarah arrived. He welcomed Sarah into his spacious home and showed her around and explained the reason for the lack of furniture before they sat down and began enjoying a beautiful dinner alone and one another's company. Carl enjoyed Sarah being in his home as they spent time talking and when she decided to leave Carl walked Sarah to her car and they kissed for only about the second or third time even though they had been out numerous times before over the past several months and had grown to really like one another and enjoyed being together. After Sarah departed, Carl began cleaning up the kitchen and washing the dishes when Betty suddenly appeared downstairs after seeing Sarah leave. She said Master Carl, as he turned to see her standing there dressed in her maids outfit and then asked what she wanted. Then asked her why, she was dressed like that. She asked why he didn't let her serve them at dinner. He said it was a private affair and it didn't involve her. She asked if he was ashamed of her, to which he said no, he wasn't and the next time he might allow her to serve his guest. He could tell her feelings were very hurt, it was obvious just by her appearance now as he asked her if there was something she needed or wanted. She replied she wanted to serve her master. Carl reminded her when she said that she was only here to serve him, don't you remember. She said yes sir, said she was scared now he would put her out since she had said that. Carl said he wouldn't put her out because of that and would let her serve his guest the next time, but she really needed to stop questioning any of his decisions. He asked if there was anything else she wanted to discuss. Betty said she needed to be punished. Carl told her to go to the basement and stand in the middle of the floor and wait. She complied and went downstairs. Carl now was starting to get really pissed off and felt if she was going to start becoming insolent, then he need to discipline her more often, beside it's what she wanted and had come to expect, besides he was trying hard not to punish her but part of him was beginning to truly enjoy it even though the thought of punishing another human was very appalling to him.

Carl knew or suspected what it really was, the same thing with most women. Betty was jealous because there wasn't a female presence here when she arrived and she was attempting to claim her position but he wouldn't and could not have any of it. He went downstairs and Betty looked very sexy in her maid's outfit. Carl walked up to her, looked her in her pretty brown eyes and said he decided that she should pack up all her clothes and documents and he would take her to a shelter, or even better get her a motel room since she had money, and until he could make arrangements for a place for her to live and a job because he was tired of her questioning him about his decisions and didn't like hitting a woman any longer, and besides, she wasn't his wife and owed her absolutely nothing. Betty dropped down to her knees as she grabbed and held his legs, just like the first time when he met her as tears quickly formed in her big brown eyes as she shook her head and pleaded with him that she wouldn't give him any more trouble or ask any more questions. Please master Carl please as she held him tightly and continued to beg as she pleaded with him. Carl then asked her to standup. Betty did as she continued crying, and asked so you want to stay here then; she said oh yes please Master Carl as he looked at her and told her you know I detest having to punish you. Said she knew he didn't like to punish her but said she needed it. Carl said I should really make you leave here. Betty screamed and cried falling to her knees again as she cried and kissed his feet, held his legs and begged him please master Carl. Carl looked down at her as she begged and cried before he told her to remove all her clothing and shoes. Betty slowly stood and began removing her maids outfit and folded it neatly and placed it on one of the bar stools. When she was completely nude Carl went to the garage and soon returned, producing a new very thin orange safety cone his workmen used when out on a job and placed it in front of Betty, this one was brand new and had never been used as he removed it from the plastic bag and handed her a tube of lubricant and told her to apply it to her vagina and anus. He said to use plenty of it as he placed the collar on her and hooked the long leash from it to one of the ceiling hooks. Then he stood in front of her and said I know what your problem is, and told her, she wasn't his wife, but his slave, because that is what you want to be, and asked her if that was true. She said yes it was Master Carl. He told her as long as she was obedient and he was satisfied with her house work she could stay here and serve him, but if she ever became a disappointment to him or became a problem which she was very, very close to becoming, or was disrespectful to him or to any of his guess in any way, shape or form she would have to go, and asked if she understood him now. He told her if she ever questioned what he did again he would not hesitate in throwing her out, and if she thought he was playing with her she would soon find out and asked her again if she understood. She replied, yes sir, Master Carl. Betty was more fearful of being put out than of being abused by him. He held her face with one hand and kissed her and said he loved her but that wouldn't matter if she failed to do what he just explained to her as he felt her between her legs and smacked her vagina hard several times and grabbing it roughly as he fingered her, she was highly excited by this now an especially when he touched her as he instructed her to start riding the safety cone. She squatted down on it as Carl went and sat at the bar and fixed a drink. Betty eased herself slowly down on the cone and Carl went and pulled out a whip. Betty noticed him as he returned to where she was and began circling her; he struck out at her and told her she was a piece of shit which seemed to make her even more excited. Carl went and pulled some small clamps out and approached Betty and placed one on each nipple and a couple on her thighs as she winced from the pain. He circled her and whipped her several more times as she sat down allowing the cone to penetrate her more deeply, it was a very, very narrow and tall cone with a smooth round tip about three feet tall and a with a ten inch diameter at the base, and Carl struck out at her fat vagina and she began climaxing and then Carl told her to now sit on it, she stood briefly before easing her anus down on the cone and soon she was enjoying it as he whipped her vagina more as she climaxed again then she played with her clitoris. He made her stop and pulled the clamps on her nipples and twisted them before removing them.

He moved the cone, unhooked the leash and told her to stand in front of him as he asked if she enjoyed that. She said that she did very much. Carl found this extremely large latex penis, it was short but attached to a harness and it also had a large anal plug and returned and inserted the butt plug easily inside her anus and then the penis inside her vagina and fastened the belt portion around her waist and fastened it all together. He placed cuffs on her wrist then attached them to the loops on the sides of the harness, placed the leash on her collar, then Carl walked her around the large basement several times as the harness did it magic on her as she was having orgasmic spasms before he then tied the leash to the ceiling hook again and took several pictures of her as she continued having organisms. He sat back and finished his drink leaving her there as he left to use the bathroom. Carl returned and decided to blindfold her and fixed another drink. Carl thought to himself, he was slowly turning into Harold, not as cruel though as he wanted to justify it in his mind what he was doing. But knew that it was Betty doing it to him, but also realized he was really enjoying what he was doing to her now as he became highly aroused, and thought how sick that was and never intended to pursue the course he was on now. He decided to let her stand there for almost an hour before he untied the leash from the ceiling and walked her around the basement again, and soon she was having several more organisms before making her kneel and open her mouth as he now pulled himself out and told her to suck him off which she expertly did until he came in her mouth and told her to swallow it all. He had her stand, removed the blindfold and looked in her face and telling her she should be satisfied now as he now saw a look of total satisfaction on her face. He removed the cuffs and then the harness and butt plug and told her to go clean everything, which she did before placing them back in the suit case when she returned. He then had her stand before him and asked her if she was happy now, she replied; oh yes sir, Master Carl, and said thank you master Carl.

He held her pretty face in one hand and kissed her, telling her she was a good slave as long as she obeyed him. Told her she would one day have a mistress to serve also and asked her if she had a problem with that, she said, no sir, Master Carl. He told her to go upstairs and shower and go to bed, because she had to finish waxing the floors and cleaning the house tomorrow, she said, yes sir, Master Carl and quickly departed.

# Six

It was several weeks later when Sarah invited Carl to dinner at her beautiful home, after arriving he was greeted by her housekeeper Yan; she welcomed him inside and said her mistress would be down shortly. And directed him into a well-appointed living room; it was very spacious, warm and very comfortable. Yan asked him if he would like some refreshments, and Carl said some water would be fine. Yan departed and soon returned with a glass of ice water, with a slice of lemon and a coaster. Yan was short and very cute, she stood about five foot one and was very petite, she had long black hair that was tied in a large bun, and she had a shapely figure and was very well proportioned for her height. She was dressed in oriental style black silk pajamas with gold trim and with beautiful oriental designs in front and back and she was exceptionally polite. Soon after Sarah appeared, Carl stood as she entered the room; they hugged and kissed as she welcomed him to her home as he complimented her on how well her decorations and accoutrements went together. Sarah was also dressed in an oriental style silk dress; it was red and blue with gold dragon embroidery. He stated he had only started decorating with his bedroom being the most important room for him because of its size and would eventually do the rest of the house over time and was in no real hurry. He had moved often in the past and that was because of his business of rehabbing homes but was going to stay in this one. Said she fully understood and asked how long he thought he might be in his current home. He told her probably much longer than before and was very satisfied with its ample space and was able to have many additional features added before it was built given he had taken over the property from a couple who wanted out of there contract, but went on to elaborate he really liked the view and privacy plus the large private acreage and was very happy with his neighbors and felt he would probably be there quite a long while now, and besides, because of its location, its where he met her.

He complimented Sarah on her house keeper, saying how polite she was. Sarah said Yan was a story unto herself, about how she had come to be here with her. Carl said he had mentioned to her about having a housekeeper also and next time she came over she would have the opportunity to meet Betty, but said he wanted to have a quiet time just with her when she had come to dinner a few weeks earlier and had made his house keeper stay in her bedroom. She showed him around her spacious home; it was very warm and cozy, not even close to being as large as his house, but very comfortable and very well decorated. Sarah said Yan had prepared the dinner for them and asked if he liked oriental cuisine. He said very much and enjoyed Chinese and Japanese cuisine and especially sushi. Soon they were sitting down together eating and the food was very delicious as she and Carl sat and ate a portion of the meal with chop sticks and was served by Yan. It was a marvelous dinner and soon they retired to the living room and talked. They talked about business and there likes and dislikes even more every time they were together and Sarah told him she thought he was a very compassionate person and she enjoyed his company very much and was feeling more attached as time passed and they spent more time together. They made plans to see a movie in the next few days and then he would have her over again at his house for a cookout later in the month during the coming long holiday weekend. Sarah said that sounded so wonderful. Soon Yan approached and said mistress; the kitchen was clean and ready for her inspection. Sarah momentarily excused herself and followed Yan into the kitchen and then Carl heard Sarah raise her voice slightly and soon heard her tell Yan to do it all over again and she would deal with her later. Sarah returned to the living room looking a little pissed and Carl asked if there was anything wrong. Sarah explained that Yan needed to be disciplined every now and then, and tonight was probably going to be a now.

Carl laughed out loud and Sarah turned to face him as she asked him what was so funny. He said it was a long story, but she might like to hear it anyway, and would try to make it as interesting as possible. Told her about his housekeeper Betty, and that she was similar to Yan except she begged to be disciplined, and said she even begged him to punish her and he found it very difficult to do at first because he didn't believe in hitting women, but had now grown to understand some people were like that and that it also played into some of his own repressed and kinky sexual fantasies. Sarah became very interested an asked how did it happen; as Carl went on to tell how and when he had met Betty his housekeeper, and their very first encounter. He explained about how she became that way over time and about the photographic and video record her husband had made and kept over the years as he subjected her to more severe and very cruel punishments and humiliation and eventually putting her photos and video of her humiliation on the inter-net. How he had now became a victim of Harold's revenge in his effort to save Betty from his abuse. Sarah was very much intrigued by the story and said that's so very interesting. Then Carl asked her why Yan calls you mistress. And Sarah went on to explained how she had received Yan as a gift from a wealthy Chinese business man and merchant whom she did taxes for and had helped along with his lawyers to help keep him out of jail by auditing his books. He eventually returned to China to avoid paying any taxes and avoiding spending any time in jail. He presented her with Yan to keep as a thank you gift, and explained she was to serve her for the rest of her natural life because she was paying off a debt her family owed him and also wanted to show Sarah his deep appreciation for her services and it was far less trouble for him to leave her, and just give her away, and said the alternative would have been death for her since she was a serious personal liability of sorts. The business man was a merchant and told Sarah, Yan was to serve her like the slave she was and could do anything to her she wanted and may even find it necessary to punish her, and if she died, it was no big deal, just don't get caught with the body. Sarah found that sometimes she had to use a cane on her, before she would act right. Carl laughed and said I bet we are the only people with submissive servant problems. They discussed how they disciplined both Yan and Betty, and Sarah said maybe they should have them together and punish them both. If Yan saw Betty being whipped she might be less trouble, or even whip her to make her even more obedient. Carl told Sarah how he had told Betty she might have a mistress one day soon and then took a big chance when he asked Sarah if she enjoyed watching pornography or bondage and discipline videos, to which she said yes. It surprised him when she said that and also said she had a few bondage videos of her own and had never discussed the subject with anyone else ever before now.

She asked Carl if he had sex with Betty. He said that so far he only had allowed her to please him orally, and found it difficult at times since she did arouse him very much but no, because he wanted to keep her at a distance since she hadn't been with him long enough yet but he did give her pleasure and described playing with her and how he ended up fisting her by accident but had never tried having vaginal or anal sex with her yet, and felt she would have to earn the privilege and how he felt she might be trying to claim a place since there was no female presence in his home before she arrived. He went on to explain further since there wasn't another woman when she arrived she might be jealous and threatened to put her out which she feared more than being punished, humiliated or even abused. Sarah said that was just amazing and asked him if she could bring Yan over and use some of his bondage equipment and she would let Carl discipline Yan if she could do Betty. Carl said that wouldn't even be a problem and would enjoy seeing Sarah whip Betty and have her serve them both. Sarah said she felt so much better now that she had someone that was even more like her than she could have imagined, and then told him she always wanted to be tied up and made love to and to have the multiple climaxes liked what he had described to her of Betty having. And had always wanted to whip and dominate another woman and make her preform on her which she made Yan do sometimes. Carl said to her he had never discussed with anyone ever looking at porn and especially bondage and discipline videos or anything sexual before now, and told her she was the very first and felt extremely comfortable around her discussing the subject. And also they hadn't had this conversation until now and were surprised the subject hadn't come up before but they understood why it hadn't. Carl said because he knew it was what he kind of considered his dark side and how many people actually have live in servants now and it wasn't something he was broadcasting.

Sarah said she felt even more comfortable with him now since having this particular discussion and invited him up to her bedroom and asked him to make love to her. Shortly afterwards they went upstairs and Sarah asked him to please discipline her, and Carl asked for the belt from her robe after they had kissed and undressed. Sarah was extremely beautiful and even more so in the nude, as Carl began first by rubbing her down with some massage oils she had as he felt her soft smooth body all over as she then became highly excited, he whispered in her ear how he was going to ravage her body as he felt between her thighs and she suddenly became overly excited since it had been several years since having sex

111

with a man as he played with her and lightly bit her neck and she became so aroused and wet she just all of a sudden erupted having a massive orgasm. She began panting as he gently bit, licked and tickled her hard erect nipples with his tongue sending shivers through her sexy body as he slowly slid down between her soft smooth thighs and inhaling her sweet sent as he now firmly held her ankles with both hands as she attempted to close them as he rubbed his chin into her shaven and very clean vagina and licked her clitoris while rubbing his chin with its short whiskers around her vagina, sending spasms through her again as he began to part her pussy lips with his tongue and massaging the inside of her vagina with his tongue, and then pushed the hood back from her clit with his tongue and licked her as she now erupted over and over again as he continued to firmly hold her ankles as she shook continuously with unending organisms, before he climbed on top of her, pinning her arms down above her head and telling her how he was going to fuck her hot wet sweet pussy as she moaned and he entered her slowly since she was tight but very wet, then after several long slow deep strokes he rammed it deep inside of her as she screamed, and hollered, oh yes fuck me, yes please fuck me again she screamed, as Carl then reached around and fingered her anus as she responded wildly and climaxed over and over again as she held on to him tightly. He then wiggled his finger around her anal opening before easing it deeper inside her as she cried yes fuck me as he continued pumping her very hot pussy. Then Carl pulled out and raised her thighs up and slowly slid his penis up into her now open but very tight anus as she cried and soon she came again as he played with her clit and then he came as the head of his penis penetrated deeper inside her tight anus, filling her anal cavity with a massive amount of his very hot and very pent up sperm as he played with her clit some more before pulling out and laying down beside her. She reached over and held him tightly as they lay like that for several long minutes quietly petting one another until both had slowly recovered. She rolled on top of him as he held her butt with both hands and he said I didn't get to tie and spank you up yet.

She told him that was the greatest sex she had ever had, she had several orgasms and had never been this sexually excited and satisfied before. She kissed him all over before they went and showered together then she took him in her mouth and he came again as she licked him, he then gave her a golden shower before they bathed one another. They soon were drying off and then laid back down and began oiling one another as he felt her body all over and she began to become aroused again and she then massaged him. She told Carl she didn't feel uptight any longer and was happy she had finally made love to him, and told him how she became so excited every time she had been with him after they first met. But felt she needed more assurances about him before having sex because she didn't want her feelings hurt, even though she had masturbated several times while thinking about him and said she was sure now after their conversation this evening more so than ever before. He told her how wonderful and pleasurable it was and felt less tense and uptight also because having Betty around, and her being nude was getting to be too much to bare as he repressed his strong sexual feeling. She asked him if he wanted to spend the night, and he replied, he would love too but only if he had known earlier before coming over so he would have been more prepared. Thanked her, but said he had a full day ahead of him tomorrow and needed to go home and get some rest now after having sex with her. And stated if he stayed, they would never get any rest because he would be all over her. Carl said they should plan ahead and then we can have Yan and Betty entertain us as we enjoy their love of punishment and pain. Sarah said that sounds so very exciting. He told her he had never pictured himself being a master, it just happened that way. Sarah suggested that we should get some of those leather pants and vest with the black boots as we watch them and put them through their paces. He reached over and began rubbing her again and said she loved his touch, and now that they had made love she wanted to see him much more often than they had been before. He said he felt the same way and said he was falling very much in love with her now since they had many shared and common interest. They kissed and Sarah said she loved him already and had been looking for a man like him for a very long time that she could share her most personal and deepest inner feeling and secrets with.

He looked at the clock and said it had gotten pretty late and he really needed to head home. Carl started to dress and before he could start she asked him to feel her again before leaving. He pressed her against the bedroom wall and held one of her arms behind her back and felt between her thighs and told her he would spank her hard next time if she wasn't a good girl and spanked her pussy lightly several times as she climaxed again as he continued to play with her, releasing her arm and fingered her ass again also causing her to have another massive orgasm. He finally released her but had to hold her because her knees began to buckle, and hugged her tight, she hugged him also and kissed him silently and then said she loved him. He released her, and went and washed his hands again before dressing. She then put on her robe and walked him downstairs, where they kissed each other good night and Carl departed.

When Carl arrived home after pulling inside his garage, sat in the car a few minutes as he brought up the home camera app scanning through the various hidden cameras throughout his large house, and found Betty asleep in her bed naked with her legs spread wide open and one of the large dildos lying beside her. Carl thought she probably had gotten hot and needed a release. But then he thought about it even more now, she hadn't asked his permission, he would have to do something about that. He got out and unlocked the back door after closing the garage door and went upstairs to his bedroom and undressed and got comfortable before he checked on Betty. He went and opened the door to her bedroom, turning on the ceiling light, walked in and looked down at Betty as she suddenly woke up startled, she looked up at him surprised as he asked her what the dildo was doing in her bedroom. She hesitated and said she felt comfortable with it close by as he picked it up and it was sticky, really sticky and slick with her fluids and also had

115

lubricant on it, he made her spread her legs open and she was dripping wet with excretions as he reached down and felt her vagina. He told her she hadn't asked his permission to jerk herself off and asked her why she had just lied to him. She said she was very sorry as Carl made her get up and wash it off and bring it downstairs and put it away. She was naked as they both headed downstairs to the basement where he cuffed her hands in front of her before he hung her from the ceiling. He looked into her eyes and asked, what he should do to her since she hadn't asked permission, but explained to her what really pissed him off most of all was, she had just then lied to him. She was very scared now and began to shake since Carl had never punished her before without her asking for it. He walked over behind the bar where he kept the suitcase with all of the restraint equipment he had brought with her as he removed a whip and returned and made her hold it in her mouth, and then returned to the bar and fixed himself a drink, sitting down and looking at her. He said nothing as he savored and sipped the drink; as she began to perspire now with real fear. He then stood in front of her and said you know I brought you here so no one would take advantage of you, you volunteered to serve me, and to obey me, but you cannot be trusted to behave even when I am away. You could at least have cleaned up after yourself and I would have never known, then on the other hand maybe you wanted me to find you like I did. He removed the whip from her trembling mouth and asked her to explain.

She said that since he was gone, thought it would be alright if she took herself since she needed to be satisfied and since he hadn't used her and she felt bad about not satisfying him and thought he would be ok with it. He told her you didn't ask permission and that isn't what I am most upset about Betty, it's because you just lied to me about it. She said yes Sir Master Carl, and said she was very sorry. He asked her what she thought he should do about it. Betty said she didn't know but whatever he decided she deserved. Carl said to her I really felt sorry for you as I watched the videos of you over the years and felt you needed some love, but now I see you don't deserve any compassion. I won't throw you out but I will have to punish you because of this, as he grabbed her pussy, then her ass, and then as he held her head said to her, you belong to me now, do you have a problem with that. She said no sir master Carl. He felt between her legs and played roughly with her until she climaxed. So what should I do to you as he looked in her fear filled eyes? He released her and removed the cuffs and returned the whip and cuffs to the case. And told her to sit at the bar and he fixed her a drink and himself another and he asked her did she like being the way she was now. Betty replied, she didn't know how to be any other way now and liked her life even more now with him and wanted to serve Master Carl. He said you remember how you got to be this way don't you. She said, yes sir, and said she deserved it because she was stupid and needed instruction. He told her to drink up and she did, and then told her she would soon have a mistress for the second time and that she would have to serve her also, and asked her if she was ok with that again. She said yes master; as long as I was here she would be happy to serve us both and looked forward to it. Carl said she will punish you also if you are disobedient and how do you feel about that. Said it would be ok because she deserved to be punished whether she was bad or the master or mistress desired it. Betty said she would be happy to serve me and the mistress, and would be loyal and obedient to both. She finished her drink and Carl made her another, she drank it slowly as Carl looked at her, then asked her when she was called names did that excite her, she said yes sir, it made her feel wanted because she was still here and deserved it, because she was a stupid bitch. He said you like being abused don't you. Said she had grown to love it because she was free of any worries; all she had to do was to serve her master or mistress.

Carl then ordered her after she finished her drink to stand with her hands on top of her head in front of him as he took her nipples between his fingers and squeezed them gently and asked her what she felt like doing now. Said she wanted to please her master anyway he wanted. Carl told her to shower and go to bed but to crawl to her bedroom, he had enough and needed some sleep and didn't have any more time to waste on Betty tonight.

When he returned to his bedroom after watching Betty crawl he checked his phone and there was a text from Sarah. Said she had the most wonderful time and when he received it to call her which he did. She wondered what had happened to him and he explained to her what had happened and said instead of punishing her he talked to her and she was a total submissive, and wanted to be punished. Told Sarah whenever you want that she could come over and he was sure she would like having Betty serve her. Sarah said they would talk soon and wished him a very good night and said she loved him. Carl climbed into bed and quickly went to sleep.

The following week was busy as usual for Carl, purchasing four more homes that were sold together in a block sale; they were well constructed but had been vacant for several years and needed a lot of work to become habitable. He had them stripped down completely and replaced all the electrical, some of the plumbing, all the windows and the roofs were completely replaced and new and larger porches added, with updated modern kitchens and bathrooms since they were brick and built in the early fifties. The neighborhood was coming back to life and Carl bought several nearby vacant lots and soon had new construction going up close to and near his many rehabs as he worked with other contractors for his newly constructed homes. New and improved he would say as he handed off sales to a sales associate in his new real estate office operation and marketed them directly, making a huge profit and soon out of fourteen rehabs and twenty six new constructions he would make a bundle over the next few months as people looked for very affordable housing which he made a point of supplying.

Several days later he and Sarah went to the movies and enjoyed each other's company and began making plans for a holiday weekend together at his house. Sarah would bring Yan and then they could enjoy each other even more having Yan and Betty serve them both together.

Carl had an above ground pool installed right off his deck and bought some very comfortable patio furniture and a charcoal grill since he wasn't crazy about gas grills for outdoor cooking because the meats just didn't have that smoked flavor. He had also purchased a few more home furnishings and several more items from an oriental furniture store because he liked the extremely large vases and the oriental styles as he added more large area rugs of Persian origin and designs as it gave the house a much warmer felling even though it still seemed very sparsely decorated because of the large size rooms. Two of the large bedrooms remained completely empty but did install window treatments, but Carl had also purchased a nice size dining room table that could seat eight and it sat on a large Persian carpet and he even added a few pictures to the dining room walls, including a couple of large abstracts, but he wasn't in no particular hurry to furnish the house right away, he had plenty of time.

# Seven

The holiday weekend was quickly approaching as Carl and Sarah began planning for the long weekend they would spend together, starting early on Friday morning all the way until late Monday evening. There intentions were being together having fun, sex, cooking and also having both Yan and Betty serve them. Sarah asked Carl where Yan would be sleeping. Carl replied she would bunk with Betty, since she had her own room and slept in a queen size bed. Sarah said that would be just great because Yan slept on a traditional oriental bamboo mat on the floor in one of the large closets she converted that she used as her bedroom and if she needed, could roll it up and bring it with her if it was necessary. Carl said it wasn't because Betty had more than enough room for Yan in her bedroom. That Friday morning, Sarah called Carl early and said she was on her way over, Carl told her he would leave a garage door open for her and to park inside whenever she arrived, she thanked Carl and they soon ended their call. It wasn't very long after the phone call before Sarah and Yan arrived a little before noon, she parked inside of Carl's spacious garage since he only had the one car and the garage could hold up to four cars. Sarah and Yan entered the house through the back door and Carl soon introduced Betty to Sarah. Carl told Betty that Sarah was her new mistress and to do whatever she was asked or told and to treat whatever her request were as if it was him telling her, and asked her if she understood. Then turned to Betty and said, and what do you say slave, Betty said yes sir master Carl, and yes

Mistress Sarah. Sarah instructed Yan that Carl was her master now also and to do whatever he instructed her to do, and asked if she understood, she said yes mistress and yes sir master Carl. Carl instructed Betty to take Yan upstairs to her bedroom because she would be staying in her bedroom with her. He instructed Yan that she was to sleep in the bed while she was here and not on the floor, and reminded her that if he found her sleeping on the floor she would be severely punished for being disobedient and disrespectful. She said yes sir master Carl, and told Betty to take Sarah's bags upstairs and place them inside his bedroom. Carl took Sarah upstairs on the elevator as Betty and Yan used the stairs. Carl showed Sarah to his bedroom, and she was amazed at its extra-large size and yet it was warm and very cozy. They began hugging and kissing and started feeling on one another right away and Sarah said she was so very horny right now. They both quickly undressed each other and Carl pushed her onto the bed and she almost climaxed as soon as he began touching her, as he grabbed her ankles and spread her legs wide open and spanked her vagina causing her to have a massive organism right away, and as soon as he began fingering her she began to lose all of her self-control, as she tried very hard not to. Carl began talking to her dirty as he slid his hard penis into her now very moist vagina as she began going wild and had the most massive climax ever as she held on to him for dear life as he continued to slowly pump her hot and now very wet pussy before he pulled out and turned her over and pulling her butt up as she knelt with her head down, penetrating her vagina again as he began spanking her ass cheeks and reaching around, holding her and rubbing on her clit before he began pulling, pinching and twisting her now very sensitive nipples, as he held her, she continued to have repeated orgasms and then he fingered her hot anus and began working, first one finger and then two and very soon after had three fingers inside of her before sticking his now very large and hard manhood into her now welcoming anus and slowly working it in and out before he shortly climaxed inside her anal cavity filling it with his hot semen, this time she hollered and shortly they both collapsed as Carl rolled over on his side next to her.

She turned to face Carl, and grabbed his face in both her hands, kissing and licking him all over for a long time as he held her before they were able to regain some strength as he then pulled her up and led her to his very large and spacious bathroom where they showered together for a long time sitting on the bench kissing using the rain feature. Sarah really enjoyed being in his spacious bathroom with the bidet and complimented him on how very clean everything was. He said yes, he had Betty clean his bathroom every day along with all the other bathrooms. She complimented him on having such an obedient housekeeper. When they had finished bathing Sarah said she was now very hungry. Carl said he had prepared a lunch, and it was waiting for them downstairs. They dried themselves off before they went and applied some body lotions to one another before they dressed and went downstairs where they found Betty peeling potatoes and Yan helping her clean the vegetables. Carl removed some sandwiches he had made earlier from the refrigerator and a chilled bottle of California red wine and brought it all over to the kitchen counter while he and Sarah sat in the comfortable hi backed stools and ate and drank the wine. They watched Betty and Yan do the prep work for a potato salad, and a pasta salad that he would make when they were finished. Sarah said the house had a much warmer feeling now than before. Said he had purchased some furniture so it wouldn't seem so empty and wasn't in a real rush to decorate and had decided to stay put this time since he had spoken to her about it last and decided to make this his home and staying in one place for once. Said he had grown really tired of moving it seemed so often and because he couldn't acquire some of the things he really liked, and besides he was getting older and was becoming more settled now and felt his overall outlook on a lot of things was changing. Said he had bought some additional patio furniture adding to what he already had and giving him some additional seating choices along with the above ground pool he had installed because he liked to swim especially when it's really warm outside. He asked her if the sandwich was enough because she could have another or they could split one if she wanted more. They decided to share another one between them. After they finished, they walked out on the deck and relaxed for a short while as Sarah said to Carl that he hadn't tied her up yet, she wanted to experience being subjected to being helpless and dominated and would feel safe with him doing it based on what he had told her about his treatment of Betty. Sarah told him she felt he was a very compassionate person and felt very safe and secure with him; she hugged him and said she really loved him very much.

Carl said he had something she might really enjoy and told her about the cell phone controlled vibrator and how it drove Betty over the edge while hanging from the ceiling, Sarah said she wanted to try it right now. Carl suggested he needed to make the salads first and then they would play and he would fulfill all her wishes. They decided to go back inside as Betty said everything was ready. He instructed Betty as she mixed the ingredients together and he added the seasonings, and soon they were finished and he placed the salads in large plastic containers with sealing tops inside the refrigerator. He told Betty and Yan to clean up the kitchen, then go clean the upstairs and for Yan to help Betty. They both said yes sir master, as he and Sarah now headed downstairs to the basement. Carl pulled out the suitcase, opened it and retrieved the dildo as he placed his cell phone on the bar. Sarah said she wanted the full treatment, wanted him to talk to her in a degrading manner and tie her up and spank her. Carl looked at and held her, kissed her and said you are insatiable as he kissed her again and said he was only doing it because he loved her, and because she was asking for it. He caught her off guard and totally by surprise when after releasing her from his loving arms, said in a very commanding voice, undress you dirty stinking bitch. She was shocked, and caught so off guard it frightened her, but did as she was told. Then he said slowly you stupid cunt, Sarah began getting highly excited as she undressed as Carl brought out the collar and cuffs, placing them on top of the bar in front of her.

When she finished undressing, Carl ordered her to stand before him, hands at her sides as he walked around her, viewed and inspected her naked body and looked her in the eyes, and told her she was his slut bitch now, and that she needed to learn how to obey properly, or you will be severely punished.

Carl then placed the collar around her neck. Sarah had never experienced being subservient to anyone ever before, and had only masturbated and imagined herself being submissive a lot of times thinking about it and how it would be and now it was really happening to her for the very first time and she was getting highly excited and very frightened at the same time, she began trembling and shaking with fear of the unknown as moisture began to appear on her smooth skin. Carl could tell she was highly excited as her nipples began to swell and harden with excitement and stood out. He told her to hold her arms out in front of her as he placed the cuffs on her wrist, and then ordered her to place her arms behind her back, as he hooked them together; she was very excited as she pressed her knees together. He attached a leash to her collar as he said she was his bitch now and was to do whatever she was told. He retrieved the phone activated dildo and told her to spread her legs; she was so excited that when he touched her pussy she just about had a massive climax. Carl sensed it and told her she couldn't come without his permission as he very gently inserted the dildo inside of her, and said if she did she would receive a severe whipping because it would be considered being disobedient. He then took the leash and walked her around the large basement and by the time he had returned to the bar where they started from Sarah was begging him to let her climax, he told her she wasn't asking in the proper manner a slave should when addressing her master, she said please master, please may I come, please master, please. He pulled the leash and looked into her eyes and saw she was doing all she could not to, and said the slave can come, and her knees bent as she climaxed just then as he held the leash and told her to stand as she was rocked by a massive organism. He removed a section of the chain and hung it from one of the ceiling hooks. Then he released her arms from behind her as she fell into his arms and he kissed her and said he wasn't through with her bitch ass yet, she began trembling again as he cuffed her arms together in front of her and raised them up above her head and attached them to the chain. He let her hang there as he left and brought out another pair of cuffs, these were for her ankles and took out a piece of rope for her knees. After cuffing her ankles and expertly tying her knees together he went and sat at the bar and looked at her. He brought up the vibrator app and turned it on low as he watched her slowly become highly aroused again and took out two extra-large clothes pins and walked over to her and said you are my slut bitch and licked her face, as she tried to kiss him back he attached the clothes pins to her hard nipples. She winced and squirmed from the intense sensation and from being in such a precarious situation and in a very highly aroused state. The vibrator was taking its told on her as she climaxed again, and he said you didn't ask permission as he smacked her ass with his hand as she climaxed again. He whispered in her ear that since she had shown a real lack of self-control that maybe the whip would teach her how to learn to obey. She then pleaded with him that she would be good. He said you haven't learned to address me correctly you stupid ass bitch, so now I see what I must do, you will be punished more severely now, you stupid ass cunt.

Sarah was losing all of her self-control as Carl turned the vibrator up a little more and pulled a long flogger whip from the suit case, and said that her bitch ass needed to be taught how to properly address him. He twisted and pulled the clothes pins before he removed them as her nipples became even more sensitive as the sensations returned as he licked, sucked, and bit them lightly as she began to have another organism. Her breathing became short and ragged as her body glistened with sweat, he stood back and whipped her lightly all over as she then began having another even more intense organism as her whole body was wracked with the pleasurable sensations and the fear of not being in control. Carl laid the whip on the bar and turned off the dildo. He came over, kissed her and held her face in one hand as he lightly slapped and rubbed her now quivering body. He asked if she had enough, yes sir master, and please Master I will be very good as he untied her knees and removed the cuffs from her ankles, then removed the dildo as she shook and climaxed again with even more sexual pleasure. He unhooked her arms as she fell into his arms, he held her several minutes and said in a halting voice she loved him so very, very much. He removed the cuffs and collar as she kissed him and saw he was hard and got down on her knees and pulled his shorts down and took him in her warm mouth swallowing all of his manhood and soon he climaxed and she swallowed and licked him clean as he rubbed her head. He raised her up and they kissed and felt on one another. She told him that she had never had such an exciting and fulfilling experience as that before today, and said she wanted him forever. He led her to the full sized basement bathroom and there they showered together again for a second time, suddenly he bent her over, holding her arms behind her and entered her wet vagina as she continued climaxing, then he applied some shower jell to her anus and lathered her as he worked several fingers inside of her before sliding himself deep inside her now very relaxed anus, pressing her against the wall, playing with her quivering pussy as she screamed from having more continuous orgasms and she urinated as she lost all control. After he came, they showered and soon finished bathing. Sarah could hardly standup as he dried her off with a very large plush towel. They held one another and Carl had a couple of large thick robes available and wrapped Sarah lovingly in one.

Carl led the now very near total exhausted Sarah to the bar, placing her on a bar stool and fixed her favorite drink, a rum and coke, with a cherry, her wet hair was wrapped in a small towel as she sat totally exhausted and very weak from the new exciting and prolonged sexual pleasure she had just experienced. She looked up at Carl, reached out and held his hand, kissed it and told him he was her master and she was madly in love with him and never loved anyone else ever before like she loved him now. She then looked at Carl, and out of the clear blue asked if he would marry her. Carl looked at her and being so taken by surprise again, just stood up and kissed her. He looked at her and said are you serious. Carl asked her if he heard her correctly, and asked her if she was sure this is something you really want to do. Yes she replied, oh yes please, I really want to marry you that is what I truly want, she replied, and said more than anything else. Carl asked her again if she wasn't letting her vagina think for her like a man would his penis. And she replied she was positive it was what she really wanted. Then said to him yes, because no one had ever taken her heart, soul, pussy and ass the way he just did and she knew he loved her also. Carl said he loved her to, and said it would be an honor to have her as his wife. He stated Yan and Betty would have to be a part of their household because they had both made commitments to each one in different ways. Sarah said she understood that and would never ask him to put her out and understood how very dependent she was on Carl and Yan on her. They finished their drinks and Carl and Sarah went upstairs on the elevator to his bed room as Betty and Yan were just finishing cleaning up his bedroom and bathroom.

He and Sarah sat on the couch in his bedroom and held one another and discussed when they would tell their two dependents of their plans. Sarah said not until they had a chance two instill some serious discipline first, because she wanted Yan to be whipped by her new master first, saying when she was sent to her that she was told to punish her frequently and on a regular basis, but she had been very lacking in that regard. He asked Sarah if she had a problem with him having sex with Yan and having her service him. She said she was hoping he would, to make her more loyal and suggested them having her together. Carl looked at her and said you are so much freakier than I ever would have thought; she laughed and said because of him, she felt truly free now to enjoy the things she thought she would only be left to enjoy on her own and in her vivid imagination. They hugged each other and kissed as he felt her and said they needed to oil themselves, which they did and then afterwards they laid down and took a brief but well deserved nap.

# Eight

After taking the short and much needed nap together while lying together in one another's arms Sarah and Carl woke up and just laid in bed just looking at one another a long time as he stroked and caressed her head. Carl said how he was so very happy and taken by surprised when she asked him for his hand in marriage. He was also extremely happy now that he had met her and she really was the girl of his dreams. Sarah said he had turned out to be the man of her dreams also, and had always wanted to be and feel free with her vivid imagination and most of all her body, that he had rocked her world beyond anything she had ever imagined and told him she would be foolish to let a man that satisfied her the way he did slip through her hands. He then asked her if she ever questioned why certain things happen the way they do, if she believed in fate, or pre-determined destiny. She said it had crossed her mind several times in the past but never really had any deep lasting thoughts about it, before she then asked him what he was trying to say. He then told her very often thoughts about what he had experienced weighed on his mind and even his conscious as he pondered over the thoughts of why objects or even people were placed in his path of life. Said she loved him and was glad he was on her path. He reached over and pulled her to him holding and kissing her as he felt and squeezed her butt cheeks and she moaned at the pleasurable sensation of being held in his strong arms. He told her they really needed to eat something now and especially before having their way with Betty and Yan; she said yes that sounds so wonderful.

Getting dressed Carl showed Sarah the camera app and informed her that Betty didn't know about the video surveillance inside the house and preferred that she never know and to never mention it to either one of them since it was his way of keeping a check on them. They observed them both cleaning the empty bed rooms and bathrooms down the hall. Sarah said she understood and thought it was a great way of watching them. She said those bedrooms are completely empty. He said yes and would show her after they dressed. When they left his bedroom they walked around the balcony and a short distance around the hallway to one of the empty bedrooms. Sarah said they are so large and have their own bathrooms and walk-in closets; they were both similar in size as she looked at both bedrooms and said they were such wonderful airy and light filled spaces. He said you're thinking of moving in now aren't you, she blushed, smiled and said yes, you know it and told him she wanted to be with him more than anything, and it would make more sense now. Carl agreed and said great. He wouldn't have to buy anymore furniture or be concerned about decorating. Sarah laughed as they held hands and headed downstairs. Carl mentioned they needed to purchase some more restraint equipment, and explained that he only had the one set of cuffs and all of the items came when he brought Betty here and had only picked up a few items afterwards like the maids outfit, some panty hose and a body suit and suggested they go to the Sexy store before he started cooking, it was still early evening just after two pm and she said sure, that sounds good to her. They returned to the bedroom so he could get his wallet and phone and some shoes and Sarah her purse and shoes.

They left shortly in her car as she drove since; she had the newer automobile as he directed her to where the store was located. It wasn't very far away and they soon arrived, it was Sarah's first time visiting the Sexy store. They entered and she was truly amazed at the wide selection of bondage equipment and restraints available, besides the usual sexy items and devices. Carl knew just what they needed and had picked out a complete set of cuffs and another collar, another leash and blindfold, along with another phone activated dildo and several butt plugs of various smaller sizes, then he found a set of plastic shackles similar to those used in jails, only made out of plastic and they were adjustable and decided on two sets. Sarah chose several different glass dildos of various sizes and shapes. She picked out some other small items and a maid's outfit for Yan in her small size. When they had finished shopping they needed a small box for all the items they had purchased after paying for them. A little more than an hour had passed when they arrived back at home and Carl asked her to wait just a moment as they sat in her car and he brought up the home camera app, looking to see what their two submissive servants were up to. He found them in Betty's bedroom napping, and showed Sarah. She asked him what did he expected to find. He said he had wondered if they were playing with each other, then they would really have to be punished for not asking permission. Told her they have to ask for permission if they wanted to pleasure themselves or each other or it would be seen as being disrespectful. Carl caught himself as he told Sarah wow, he was starting to sound like a true slave master, and she looked at him and chuckled, and said yes you are. Sarah said she agreed with him though as they proceeded to take the new equipment inside and downstairs to the basement. They then headed to the kitchen where Carl had prepared some meats the day before for grilling, as he removed them from one of the refrigerators. Carl went to lite the grill as Sarah followed, once he had a nice fire going he asked her if she wanted to go for a swim, she said sure, and would have to get her bathing suit. He said he would get his as they reentered the house and went upstairs to undress. Sarah put on her swim suit and Carl his trunks and they brought along a couple of large towels with their bathrobes as they headed back downstairs and outside to the deck and pool.

They swam for about forty minutes before they got out and Carl went inside to the kitchen to get the pan of meats, returned and started cooking. It didn't take very long for him to grille enough meats for all of them before he closed up the grill. He and Sarah went inside sitting at the booth and ate there fill. When they finished eating, Carl then brought up the camera application and spoke through it and woke up Betty and Yan and told them to come downstairs. When they appeared told them to fix themselves some food and eat, then cleanup and afterwards, when they had finished, they were to report to him and Sarah. They both replied yes sir master and went to prepare their plates.

He asked Sarah, when was the last time Yan had a physical. She replied just two weeks ago she had taken her for her annual checkup at her regular doctor. Said she was in very good health and had no medical problems or issues. Carl said very well as he and Sarah returned to his bedroom to put their shorts and t-shirts back on before returning back downstairs. Carl and Sarah went to the basement bar and he fixed some drinks and checked out the new restraint equipment they had just purchased and they together cleaned all of it first before they would use it on their lowly subjects. Carl said he now needed a cabinet to place everything in and they should shop for one, one day soon, and Sarah agreed with him. By the time they had sorted through everything Carl decided to bring out a long folding table so they could arraigned everything on it by device and who would wear what as he placed the suitcase he had brought with Betty next to it. After they had finished they sat and sipped their drinks and talked. Carl had Sarah program her phone to use the new remote dildo that they had just purchased, and she was so very excited about using it. Carl suggested she use it on herself so she would know how the different settings felt and what the sensations were like at the many different settings. Sarah used a wipe on it and then a paper towel before she inserted it into herself, and turned it on and said oh wow, and then she slowly turned it up and told Carl to hold her as she climaxed in his arms and tried to turn it down but he held her just out of reach, and she shook again before he let her stop it, she said please don't let her go yet. She soon calmed herself down and removed it, wiping it off. Carl asked her what she thought about it, she said it was just like when he did it to her and couldn't wait to do Yan or Betty. Carl said we have to build up the whole situation slowly with Yan and Betty; it's kind of like a form of theater, a slow build up to an arousing climax. They enjoyed their conversations together as they laughed and joked about various subjects and it wasn't very long before both Betty and Yan came down stairs and stood before them both.

Carl turned to Sarah and said, let the games begin. Carl told Betty and Yan to stand in front of them both. They stood before them as he began to explain they were going to have a training session so they would both understand the meaning of true allegiance an obedience that he and Sarah would expect from them both each and every day. He then stood and faced Betty and asked her what was her purpose in life, she said to serve you Master Carl and now Mistress Sarah, he said very well. Then he stood in front of Yan and asked her the same question. She said to serve Mistress Sarah and now you also master Carl. He stepped back and told them both to undress. Betty did without any hesitation because she knew what was about to happen and welcomed it, but Yan was slow and hesitated, which wasn't very good for her as Carl noticed her reluctance, and asked her if she had a problem with what she had just been ordered to do, and she meekly replied, no sir master. He said to her, what did you say slut, she said, no sir, Master Carl. He told her that was much better as the look of pure fear was on her pretty face. Carl waited until they were both completely nude and standing before him and Sarah, as he had them fold their clothes and place them in a neat

137

pile on an empty bar stool then to turn slowly around as he inspected them both very closely. He told them they were slave sluts and were here to serve and were going to experience some training. He then went to the table and picked up the collars and returned and placed Bettie's collar on her and handed Yan's collar to Sarah as she then placed it on a very fearful Yan. Carl brought over the two leashes and handed one to Sarah. Then he explained they were going to have a training session and that they were going to learn to do whatever they were told, and do it without any hesitation as he directed his attention towards Yan. Carl brought the cuffs over and told them to hold their arms out in front of them, he cuffed Yan first, then Betty. He looked Betty in her eyes and said you and Yan are now sisters and will suffer the same punishment together because that is what mistress Sarah and I have decided on, do you understand me bitch?, she replied yes sir master Carl; he stood before Yan and asked her if she understood, she said yes sir master Carl. He cuffed both their hands behind their backs and brought back the telephone controlled dildos. Carl asked Sarah to have a seat as he walked Yan and Betty around the basement and back again before he slowly inserted the dildos inside each, first Betty and then Yan. Yan was tight and knew she would really feel it much more. He sat at the bar with Sarah and they turned them on. He had Sarah do Betty, as he did Yan, they started out on a very low setting as he watched Yan's expression of total surprise and then watched as she was starting to have a hard time standing up and turned it off. He told Sarah he needed to hang them up and returned with two lengths of chain, which he then hung one length each from the ceiling hooks. He un-cuffed and then re-cuffed both women with their arms in front and then attached them to the chains hanging above their heads, as their arms were stretched above their heads. He said to Sarah now that's much better and decided to bring over the blindfolds and went to the table and returned then placed them on both Yan and Betty. He returned to the bar and kissed Sarah, she was all smiles as she watched them begin to squirm with anticipation. They toasted one another, and said one other thing he needed to do and brought back two short pieces of rope and tied both with their knees together, then he told Sarah they were now ready and turned the dildos back on, starting on low and then gradually increasing over an extended period of time as the two hung and began dancing, gasping, moaning and screaming as they were experiencing having multiple uncontrollable organisms and couldn't touch themselves as he and Sarah increased the settings and played with the controls. He then set the vibrator in Yan on pulse as they watched for a long period of time and she soon had uncontrollable organisms and was moaning very loudly and shook violently as the pulses soon began taking their toll on the petite and sexy Yan. Carl brought back some extra-large clothes pin style nipple clamps and clamped both girls' now very swollen an aroused nipples, as they protruded as each squirmed loudly.

He and Sarah sat back and watched as both Yan and Betty danced as best they could with their knees tied as the vibrations in them brought pleasure and discomfort from not being able to touch themselves. Carl walked over and brought back a whip and began whipping both all across their entire nude bodies as they tried to move but being blindfolded didn't know when or where the lashes would land. He stopped and he and Sarah turned the dildos off. Sarah said she was very excited and wanted Carl to touch her, he reached down in her shorts and she was soaking wet and soon exploded as he placed his index finger on her clit and massaged it as she screamed with pleasure. She caught her breath and he asked her if she thought they had enough, and if she wanted to whip them. She said, yes please, and took the whip and began with Betty, then Yan as Carl went and twisted the clothes pins on Betty before removing her blindfold, and then he did Yan the same way as Sarah began whipping Betty again, and after he had removed the blindfold from Yan, he then twisted the clothes pins before he removed them. He squeezed Yan firm nipples as the feelings came back and she cringed and cried. They looked at the two hanging there as he went and smacked both on their asses as they jumped and then untied their knees. Carl grabbed a heavy leather strap and unhooked Betty and had her on her hands and knees, grabbed her leash and made her crawl around the basement as he whipped her with the strap and returned and then had her kneel before Sarah with her head down on the floor and her ass up. Then he did the same with Yan before placing her in the same position. The dildos were still inserted in both. Carl asked Sarah if she was finished with them, she thought she might be. He said he wasn't, and removed the dildos from each, and then he stood before each, whipping each hard with a thin leather strap and made sure it landed on their thighs and between their legs over ten times each. He then had them stand, they both were crying, and had them fold their arms behind them, feet apart as he went and felt each between their legs. He touched and felt both until they climaxed and then placing his hand in their mouth and had them suck his fingers clean. When he did Yan she had a very explosive climax and he had to hold her up by her long hair to keep her standing as she began sucking his fingers extremely well. He returned to where Sarah was sitting with her hand in her shorts. He commanded Yan and Betty to kneel, and told Yan and Betty that he and Sarah were getting married, and they both would be serving them. They would have a home together, and they were a permeant part of their household. He asked them if they had any questions, they each said no sir master Carl. He told them to stand as he hugged Betty and she said thank you master Carl, and said she loved him and now Mistress Sarah, Sarah hugged her also as Carl hugged Yan, she was crying and said she would be very good master Carl. He had Yan and Betty kneel again and asked Sarah to remove her shorts, which she did and sit on the stool with her knees up and legs spread, she did and told Betty to serve her mistress and lick her pussy and then her ass, Betty did as she was told and Sarah was ecstatic as Betty soon brought Sarah to a rousing climax and he told her to lick her dry and lick her ass as well. Sarah told her to please stop and pulled Betty by the hair; she enjoyed licking Sarah's hot wet pussy and ass and didn't want to stop, and begged to please continue, as Sarah relented for a short time as Betty said she tasted so good before Sarah just couldn't take any more. Carl pulled himself out and had Yan take him in her mouth after dropping his shorts and had her lick his ass also, he finally came in her mouth and told her to swallow it all. Then pulled her up by her hair also, and Yan had a great big smile on her pretty face now, and told them to kiss each other and told Yan to lick Betty and play with her pussy and soon she had her small hand inside Betty's vagina as she had a massive climax, after that he had Betty lie on the floor and told Yan squat over her with her pussy in Bettys face and soon Yan came and shook with a rousing climax. Carl ordered each to kneel before him as he urinated on both Yan and Betty, and said they had been blessed as Sarah said she had to pee also and she urinated on the two as well while they were still kneeling. Carl then told them to clean everything up as he and Sarah went to the basement bathroom and took a quick shower together and returned to watch there servants mopping the floor and cleaning the dildos.

Carl and Sarah fixed another drink wrapped in thick towels as they watched their two naked servants clean up. When they finished he ordered them to shower and bath each other in the same bathroom he and Sarah had just used and as a reward if they wanted each other they could starting tonight until tomorrow morning, but only after he and Sarah went to bed. They said thank you master Carl and went to shower together. He and Sarah had their drinks and Sarah said she hadn't been this aroused in her life ever before. How he surprised her when he had Betty eat her and lick her ass, and said it was the wildest thing she had ever experienced and sent shivers through her like never before. They kissed and hugged and toasted one another. When Yan and Betty came out of the shower wrapped in towels, Carl told them to go to their bedroom and oil themselves and they could clean up the house tomorrow. Carl and Sarah sat and talked, saying she had never been this excited or ever experienced the thing so far they had done together ever as they soon finished their drinks and went upstairs after Carl had checked and locked up the house. He decided to go to Bettys room with Sarah following and found Yan and Betty in bed, said he had some instructions for them both, told Yan and Betty they were to bath and oil their bodies daily, maintain the highest standards of cleanest and they could have one another if they wanted but after tomorrow morning if they wanted to pleasure themselves or each other they need permission from either Sarah or him, he asked if they understood. They both replied yes sir, Master Carl. Told them good night and closed their bedroom door. He and Sarah went to his bedroom and she asked him to hold her, he did as she melted in his arms and told him how much she loved him, they laid down and she asked him to take her again, Carl felt on her as she trembled with anticipation and he had her kneel with her ass up and legs spread, with her head down, as he spanked her and after ten smacks to both cheeks he felt between her legs and she had another massive climax before he pulled her ass toward him as he entered her and soon she had lost all control again and had a continuous climax as he pulled out and grabbed her by her hair turning her around and placing himself in her warm open mouth and releasing his load, and what she didn't swallow he rubbed all over her face. Then he pulled her up and kissed her as he placed a hand between her legs as spasms racked her now quivering and relaxed body. Sarah was totally spent as Carl laid her down and retrieved a warm damp wash cloth and wiped her beautiful face with the warm cloth, she was more than satisfied as they lay in bed and she curled up under him and they both fell into a deep sleep after an exhausting day of carnal pleasure.

# Nine

The following morning, really closer to ten o'clock when everyone finally woke, Carl and Sarah held each other and after relieving themselves and returning to bed, Carl petted Sarah as she curled up in his arms and said for the first time in her life, she truly felt fully sexually satisfied and felt she would now be able to accomplish so much more in her life now that she had found her true love. And told him how much she loved him as she looked at his handsome face and into his eyes. Said what he had said about fate yesterday, she felt was so very true and that it was meant for them to be together. Carl held and felt her, as she again became aroused and begged him to please stop baby, said she couldn't take it any more right now as he continued to rub on her as she began shaking as her body was rocked by another massive orgasm as she struggled to calm herself before saying in a low voice she was starving. He looked at the clock and it was close to noon as he kissed her. She gasps trying to catch her breath, and said that some food would help quite a bit since they had been so very active. They dressed putting on their shorts and t-shirts and washed up and went downstairs and found Betty and Yan were waiting for them to wake up and were prepared to fix breakfast for them both. Betty and Yan seemed very happy as they greeted them, and thanked them for yesterday. Carl and Sarah noticed that they seemed to look more refreshed and both appeared even happier. Carl asked Betty if there was anything he should know about. Betty answered him and said yes sir Master Carl, thank you for yesterday and thank you for Yan, that they loved being together with one another, and were extremely happy to be serving him and the mistress. Yan bowed and thanked Sarah for punishing her, said she really needed it, and now felt more loved. They turned and began preparing a beautiful breakfast for him and Sarah and had set places for them at the dining room table.

Carl and Sarah sat down as they were served like royalty and enjoyed their food. When they finished eating Carl went into the kitchen and kissed both Betty and Yan, thanking them both for such a wonderful breakfast and being so attentive, and then proceeded to take his vitamins. He and Sarah went outside, sitting on the deck and Carl wondered what had brought that on. Carl told Sarah he would be right back, and checked his phone and placed it on charge before returning to the deck with Sarah. Sarah asked him if anything was the matter and he said no. Then he asked if there would be any advantages if he hired her company to do his audits and prepare his company's taxes. She said maybe, and welcomed the additional business, that would be great for her and thanked him for being a new customer for her growing firm. She told him she had eleven employees and the office space was very cramped and she would soon have to move but hadn't found a suitable space at what she felt was a fair and reasonable price and really didn't want to move in with him until she had her office situation squared away first because it was so very important to her since her lease was up and the landlord was increasing the rent and the location wasn't convenient for her any longer. He said he fully understood and asked her if she had looked for a new location and how much space she needed. She described the location where she was located at now, and said the rent had gotten to be way too expensive and really out of hand for the size of the space she occupied and she didn't need the main street exposure for the type of business that she was in. The area had changed since she first moved in and started her business and had chosen that location at the time because the rent was cheap and there were several empty store fronts at the time and the leasing agency was trying to fill the empty spaces now because it was a strip mall and more of a shopping type area, it was turning out to be a real problem for her now since many of the shops had changed and generating more business and there were no longer any vacancy's since she first moved in and located her business there. She now needed a much quieter and less congested place with plenty of space for all of her records and with the ability to be able to expand without moving and she also needed good high speed internet connections and another thing she needed was less congested but ample and decent parking. She had also looked at a couple of office suites but they were much too expensive for what they offered and decided to stay where she was until she could find something she felt well suited for her situation, since the landlord hadn't upped the rent yet even though she was on a month to month right now but didn't know how long that would last. He asked if he could see her current location and he might just have the perfect space for her, and she might really like, and if not close, almost being rent free only if it suited her purpose, and it definitely wasn't cramped, but would have to be set up for her needs first because it was totally empty.

She became very excited at the prospect and wanted to see it today if it was at all possible. Carl said he had to first place the self-cleaner in the pool and then they would go take a look. After he placed the droid into the swimming pool and checked the filter and water quality, they both took a quick shower together before oiling one another, he enjoyed massaging her very shapely body with the oils, when he started oiling her after the shower and held her pretty foot in his hand. Then placed one of her toes in his mouth as she screamed as she lay on the bed begging him to please stop, she was panting and said please let her regain some of her strength back, please Carl, please baby stop. He massaged her as she used all her strength to maintain her composure until he finished, then she did him and he really enjoyed her hands on him. Soon they were dressed and she was looking so cute and very beautiful with her slim but very shapely figure. She wore a pair of knee length pants and a top with ruffled sleeves and collar, earrings and a matching necklace with medium two inch heeled sandals. Carl wore a light weight cream colored summer suit with a light blue t-shirt and a pair of boat shoes.

They went in her car since it was the newest and a luxury model and he liked riding in the new cars as he observed all the new features they offered. About fifty minutes later they pulled up and parked near her office, it was as close as they could get as they had to walk a short distance before getting to her office door. She said look at all the cars as he observed the parking lot. Carl commented it was also Saturday you know. Her office was near the end next to a dental office on one side and a clinic on the other, and the remaining business were all consumers oriented also with a fairly large clothing store, dry cleaners, and of course a dollar store and ending with one of the large chain drug store. She said her lease had run out two months prior and she was renting now on a month to month basis and it was two thousand dollars a month and they wanted five hundred more a month if she was to stay and to sign a new lease. It was the reason this was of the upmost importance to her now and hoped he understood her dilemma, he said he really did. They walked up to the front door and she unlocked and opened it, and it was a much smaller space than what he had ever imagined, it would be very tiny compared to what he was prepared to offer her and had in mind. He walked to the back and looked at the small cramped washroom and outside of that the counter where there was a coffee pot. Carl turned and said he had seen enough and asked about the banker boxes, said she was looking for a new location and had her employees packing up the unneeded older records up in anticipation of a move very soon. Carl also said the rent increase seemed to him as an indirect way of making her have to move, or what he would call a soft eviction. He said ok let's go sweetheart and gave her directions to his office and it didn't take her long to find it or to get there, as he told her he didn't use all the space he had available and it was the reason he could offer it to her next to almost rent free, and since she would soon be his wife he would be able to watch her more closely, as he then began to laugh and became very tickled. It wasn't too far away from where her current location was and had and extremely large parking lot and it could hold over one hundred autos easily as he directed her to park in his reserved spot. She was amazed at the size of the building. She commented on the sign that marked off his parking space at the front door with his name on it and said really, he laughed again as they stepped out of the car and started up the walkway past the beautiful landscaped exterior as Carl removed his keys and unlocked and opened the large glass door for her. There was a double entrance as he held the second door for her before entering the long, wide hallway and to one side a beautiful and wide, winding spiral staircase going upstairs. The hallway was wide and had very large plants on both sides and at the end of the long wide hallway about two hundred feet away was an elevator and above after walking the first ten feet or so the ceiling opened up and was two stories high with a glass atrium type ceiling and the wide interior hallway area was completely flooded with sun light for the entire length of the hallway and you could look up and see there was office space above on both sides. On the lower level on one side was his different business offices, one was labeled administration, then it was followed by the different departments, electrical and plumbing supply offices, and then the next office area was his construction and rehab operations offices, and then finally his real estate operation, across the hall was a very large empty office space and then a small area that was used as a lunch room with about a half dozen picnic style tables, several different types of vending machines and a counter top with several microwave ovens, and there was a hot-cold water dispenser, as they continued they passed another large office space that was completely empty and finally they reached the end of the hallway at the elevator. And behind the elevator she saw even more office space and a men's and women's washroom and had the appearance and feeling of being in a mall. He took her up on the extra-large elevator to the second level where it opened up into one very large open space separate only by the hallway atrium opening that allowed you to look downstairs into the hallway and that was twenty feet in front of you and was surrounded by a glass wall, then there were the very large spaces on both sides that were completely empty with very high thirty foot ceilings that gave the space such an airy and open feeling. She could see past the elevator to the washrooms which were clearly marked men and women's as she walked over and went inside the women's and was surprised by the size and layout before she went and looked inside the men's. Behind the elevator was similar to downstairs with more open space and a wide hallway leading to a set of double doors marked exit.

Sarah asked him who owned this beautiful building. He answered and said, I do and the rest of the building was his very large warehouse and storage facility for his electrical and plumbing supplies company and space for the materials used in his rehabs and his air-conditioning company. She walked around the large open space with it large floor to ceiling windows with solar shades and then he took her to another very large open space behind the

elevator as they walked down the hallway a short
distance to the double doors as they reached the back
wall and he opened one of the wide doors and they
stepped out onto a landing very high above the
warehouse floor close to the roof and you could view the
entire warehouse operation and all the vast space below
and see the rows of industrial shelving filled with pipes
and other supplies, and commented on how very huge it
was. The landing led to some stairs and was also an
emergency fire escape. They went back inside to the
office space and the door automatically closed behind
them. Carl looked at Sarah and asked her what she
thought about the space, as he repeated again it's almost
rent free. She hugged him and asked if she could look at
the empty space downstairs also. Carl said sure as he
showed her another wide stairway a short distance away
behind a set of double doors off to the side, but they rode
downstairs on the elevator. They walked the short
distance as he opened the double glass doors to the very
large empty office space downstairs and the lights came
on automatically which surprised her as he explained he
had upgraded the entire building with the latest and most
modern energy efficient lighting, electrical and climate
controls available. She noticed the only windows were on
the hallway side, but the space was extremely large and
again with a very high ceiling that allowed the sun light
to penetrate the large space and it also had its own
separate washrooms for men and women and they were
very spacious inside. Sarah asked about washrooms
upstairs, and he said there were some above the ones
down here and on both levels and explained there were

some more public ones around the corner at the end of the hallway across from the elevators on both levels and said ten different companies used to occupy the office and warehouse space here and that was the reason there were plenty of facilities, but now it was just his company and had more than enough space if he wanted to expand his operations. She wanted to look upstairs again, he said sure, they went back upstairs. She looked and found the washrooms by the elevator and the one above the space downstairs. What was office space downstairs behind the elevator could be used as a conference room, or locker room lounge and she liked upstairs so much better and said it wasn't claustrophobic like her current space and would also give her plenty of room to expand her business now. Carl then asked, have you decided what you plan on doing, you haven't said anything.

She said yes, yes, yes, oh yes baby, I want this space on this side with the windows. They walked the length of the space, he said the utilities would be included in the rent, she said you said it was free, he said yes but she would still have to sign a lease agreement and the amount would be to cover her utilities plus ten dollars, that way it would be a legal rental, said she understood. He asked do you want this entire floor, or just the half by the windows. She said yes, just the half by the windows would be enough for now because her current space wouldn't allow her to expand. She asked if she could divide the space, he said only as long as she used modular type furniture, cubes or such, and kept it open, but the cube walls could be taller, eight or nine feet if she wanted more of a private feeling which he suggested and also had downstairs. Then he asked what she had in mind. She wanted her office to be separate from the rest, different from the way it was now. He told her the air conditioning and heating system worked best with the space being open and had been designed to function that way because of the large windows for natural light, but they had cubes with tall or higher than the average wall panels to make it a more personal space and allowed for the openness to be maintained. He said he had them downstairs and they allowed you to change the configuration because they weren't permanent walls. Sarah said she loved it and asked how soon her operation could move in. Carl said that completely depends on you, the space has been cleaned twice even thought it was empty and the carpet had been removed, the lighting is energy efficient and was up to date, and all it needed was for her to have it set up and the windows washed. He would take care of the windows, but cleaning was her responsibility and had a service that cleaned his offices. He showed her the channels in the floor for internet, and video cables and phone lines also. The floor outlets that were spaced out and covered the entire floor and said there had been cubicles here once before, and pointed out the internet service here was the fastest available and the entire infrastructure was already in place. The tile ran from the elevator to the glass wall and around it for several feet, and the rest of the area would be carpeted as it had been once before. He also said the entire warehouse roof was covered with solar panels and that lowered his power cost and there was also a backup generator so she didn't have to worry about any loss of power if the weather caused outages elsewhere.

Sarah said she would agree to his terms as they departed, riding down in the elevator, but would need time setting everything up before moving in. She would have to arrange getting new cubicles, internet and carpet. She asked him to hug her and he did as they exited the building. He locked the door and suggested they go to lunch. They headed to a quaint little restaurant for a light lunch. They arrived, entered and were shown to a booth. Carl ordered some wine for them as they looked at the menu. They ordered the same thing, broiled salmon, rice, and a salad. Sarah held his hand, and said to Carl that she had no idea his company was so large. He said it wasn't, it just looked that way, because it was a service business and the construction and rehabbing happened all by accident and that was the reason he had a real estate brokers license. She was surprised again and said what don't you do, he laughed as they sipped their wine. He asked? How soon are you thinking of relocating? Said as soon as she could make the arrangements to pack up and hire some movers and inform her employees of the new location but needed everything set up and in place first. Carl said let's say a month then, Sarah said that sounds reasonable. He said you need to have insurance on the space and he would have a reserved parking space set aside for her. And said there was a directory by the front door that he would have her company name listed on it very soon.

Their food came and they both enjoyed the food and the conversation and each other's company. Some women entered and as they were going to their table, one of them recognized Sarah and stopped to speak to her and say, hello, before they continued on to their table. Carl and Sarah finished their food and decided to have dessert, when they finished Sarah said she was ready to go. Carl paid and tipped the waitress and they departed. Sarah told him her business had been the reason why she hadn't had spent much time with him more often than before this weekend, but had wanted to be with him ever since they had first met. Sarah was still driving as he directed Sarah to the nearby Sweet Woods Mall and told her he wanted to see something before they went back home. They entered the Mall entrance and Carl held Sarah's hand and she asked what was it he wanted to see and soon after they entered and the H Stein and Sons jewelry store was close to the mall entrance and they entered. He looked around and when a salesman approached, asking if he could be of any assistance. Carl said he would like to see some engagement rings as Sarah began to blush. The salesman showed him a selection and asked if Sarah was the lucky woman, and Carl said yes she was and asked her if she saw something she liked. Sarah chose a simple but very beautiful ring with several small diamonds and tried it on. It fit her long slim finger perfectly, and Carl asked her if she was happy with it. She hugged him and said she loved him as tears formed in her eyes, and Carl told the salesman he would purchase the ring. Carl paid for it and they departed. Sarah wiped her eyes and said she was very happy as they returned to the parking lot. Sarah drove them home.

On the way Carl brought up the home camera app and scanned the house for activity and found Yan and Betty finishing there cleaning and vacuuming before they sat down to eat some noodles. They seemed to be getting along well, and Carl thought that was very good. He closed the app and enjoyed the ride home. Sarah asked him why he hadn't bought a new car. He said it wasn't important right now and didn't think he would be happy with some of the newer models he had seen and was still happy with the one he had, and anyways it didn't attract undue attention when he went to some of the property locations he visited.

Sarah pulled onto the long driveway and then into the garage as Carl closed the garage door from his phone. They entered and Yan greeted them, and asked what would they like for dinner, and what time did they want to eat. Carl looked at Sarah, she was undecided. Carl said they would let them know in a little while. He and Sarah went upstairs and undressed, and he put his shorts and t-shirt on he wore around the house and then went to wash his hands and brush his teeth. Sarah soon followed and did the same. After they had finished and returned to the bedroom she grabbed Carl, pushed him towards the bed and then on to it before she quickly climbed on top, straddling him as she lay on top kissing him all over. There was a knock on the door and he said enter. Betty entered and said Master Carl, yes Betty he replied. Asking what Yan and she should prepare for dinner. He told her to take a bag of shrimp out and thaw them like I showed you then clean them and told her what vegetables to clean and prepare and he would be down shortly. She said, yes sir master and departed. He told Sarah ever since last night Betty and Yan seem to be more attentive and more obedient. Sarah responded that was a good thing especially for Yan, and maybe because she has found out she won't be alone any longer. Carl said that could be it, he needed to take her weekly picture and check her weight later on today or tomorrow.

Sarah asked to see the photographic record of Betty, the one her husband had compiled. Carl got up and went to his desk and pulled it out as he turned on his computer laptop and waited for it to come up. Shortly after he showed Sarah the record he kept of Betty since bringing her home; she had gained about fifteen pounds over the past several months, she looked so much better now and wasn't as skinny as she once was as her breast began to fill out again along with her buttocks. She looked so much better than when Carl first met her and she also looked much happier as Sarah went through the photo record Carl had started. She said you have done a marvelous job and asked him was that her cage in the basement; he said yes and would only use it when and if she really had pissed him off. Sarah sat on the couch and was amazed by the rapid decline of Betty over the years as she began looking through Harold's photo album. He told her he was in tears when he finished watching the videos because it wasn't a game Harold was playing, or love, but down right abuse and it was a very cruel thing what Harold had done to her after he finished looking through all of them. He told Sarah it was why he sat down and talked to her and found out she had come to feel free by Harold's abuse because she only had to serve him to be happy, but said the one thing that puzzled him was near the end when Harold kept saying the end was near and he was going to get rid of the shit in his life as it was coming up to the tenth anniversary of their baby's death. Carl told Sarah he loved Betty because she was a person first of all, and Betty had told him she needed to feel wanted and had told him so, and when she wanted to be humiliated she would let him know. Last evening she was so very happy serving us. Sarah said most of this goes beyond anything she would or could have imagined anyone doing. Carl said yes it does. He said he was going to check on the food preparation and to come downstairs when she was ready and Sarah asked about the videos and he told her she really shouldn't look at them because she wouldn't be able to handle it and would become very upset if she did. Sarah insisted that she be allowed to look at them, he said ok, but remember I warned you; and pulled the book out and Sarah sat at the desk and started from the beginning as he left the bedroom and headed downstairs to cook.

Sarah started just as Carl had, since they were all numbered, but unlike Carl she basically viewed them all in semi fast forward mode. By the time she reached the seventh to tenth disc she had actually hit play several times as she became aroused watching Harold as he whipped Betty and especially when he inserted the small baseball bat. Sarah had her hand between her thighs as she soon had an orgasm and went to the bathroom to clean herself. She continued as she now felt relieved and continued in fast forward as she also periodically paused in play mode to hear the conversation and especially when Harold appeared on camera and explained his perverted reasons and actions. She heard the part when he stated he was going to make a freak out of her as she observed the suction devices, the vaginal whipping and when he sucked her clitoris inside the plastic tube. Sarah had never felt such emotional conflicts before as she watched in horror and being aroused at the same time, especially when she watched Betty exposed outside and eating out of the dog food bowls. She continued as she began crying and paused and went and washed her face, before returning. Sarah was determined to see it all as she came to the last five disc and listened to Harold as he said the end was near, just as Carl said he also heard but had no idea what he meant by it. Sarah continued to the very last disc, as she now sat and cried and had very conflicted emotional and sexual feelings as she felt on herself at the same time.

Carl arrived downstairs and began directing Yan and Betty as he watched them and told them what and how he wanted the veggies prepared. They soon finished and instructed them on what pots to use, and asked Yan to fix some rice. He started cooking and asked Betty to begin setting the dining room table for four then he added the ingredients to the pan and when he finished, let the food stand several minutes. It had been a little more than an hour and a half and was about to send Yan to get her mistress, when he looked up and saw Sarah standing and she was just crying profusely as she came over to him and he held her, and whispered in her ear and said yes he knew. He dried her eyes and then she went and hugged Betty and kissed her, and said she was very sorry. She didn't respond to Sarah as he asked Betty to pour the wine that had been chilled and had Yan hand him the dinner plates as he dished them all up and took them to the dining room. He told Yan and Betty to follow and sit down to eat with them this evening, he blessed the table and everyone ate in almost near silence because of Sarah, but everyone enjoyed the meal. When they finished he instructed Yan start clearing the table along with Betty. Sarah hadn't yet fully gotten over what she had seen earlier from watching the videos. Finally Sarah spoke; her voice was very soft and calm and said how anyone could ever be so cruel to another person. Betty returned to finish clearing the table and Sarah stood, turned and hugged her again, and said she was so very sorry. Betty said there was nothing to be sorry about, she was here to serve her and was very happy now, and then asked Sarah to please punish her. Sarah shook her head and said no she couldn't and wouldn't, and then out of no where Betty slapped Sarah hard, and said she didn't deserve to be her mistress if she couldn't or wouldn't punish her. Sarah recovered very quickly after being slapped; coming quickly out of the melancholy mood she was in. Carl was standing and watching as this all occurred, as he watched and waited for Sarah's reaction and to see just what Sarah would do. Sarah's reaction came very quickly as she looked at Betty and said you stupid ass ungrateful fucking bitch, as she slapped Betty back hard, not once, but twice as Bettys head reeled from the blows. Carl grabbed Sarah's arm as she was getting ready to hit Betty again, as her anger began to rise. Carl in a commanding voice told Betty to go downstairs and wait, which she promptly did. Carl turned Sarah around and held her as he looked into her eyes and said I warned you. Now I know you want to feel pity and compassion, but you cannot let your feeling get in the way of her personal reality, you must now punish her with the same determination that I had to learn to muster, even though I at first didn't want to do it. I found that I had to in order to maintain respect and control. You can't even back down now, she just challenged you, and I won't let you back down from what you must do to her, but I will be there with you, you must not show any pity or mercy, none what so ever, just let your inner feeling flow, do you understand me now, Mistress Sarah. Sarah looked into his eyes, and he said don't worry; she disrespected me also when she slapped you, and she will pay very, very dearly for this sign of insolence, disobedience and disrespect. You don't have to worry about that but you must understand that you, and only you can regain your respect in her mind now, you must punish her and it has to be very, and I mean very, very painful just like what Harold had done to her or else she won't respect you. You can't back down, because now you have to show her who the real boss ass bitch really is, understand me, Mistress Sarah, you have no other choice. Sarah looked at him and yes Carl. Carl hugged her and reassured her that she could do it and reminded her when she had mentioned punishing her to him.

He entered the kitchen and told Yan she would have to do everything alone as far as cleaning up, she answered, yes sir, master Carl, and when you finish you can go upstairs and shower and clean yourself and go to bed or look at television, whatever you want because you probably will be sleeping alone tonight. Yes sir master Carl she replied, as Sarah watched him giving Yan her instructions. Carl turned and hugged Sarah again and kissed her and said I love you very much, and reassured her she had to do what she didn't want to do or else because it was a matter of respect. He gave Sarah a few minutes to think about what she was about to embark on now and reminded her she must feel the pain you felt by her insubordination. They turned and descended down the wide staircase to the basement where Betty awaited the outcome of her now very stupid and challenging actions. Carl and Sarah found Betty standing where she always stood when he punished her. He stood in front of her and told her she had made the worst mistake in her life ever since being in his household after all he had done for her and he would not stand for it, and asked if she understood what he just said. She answered, yes sir, Master Carl. He said you know what is going to happen to you now, you stupid ass bitch, she replied yes sir master Carl, as he told her to undress, and told Sarah to have a seat. She undressed and folded up her clothes which Carl took from her and placed on a bar stool. He went to the table and brought back the collar and a pair of cuffs and placed the collar around her neck, and told her to hold her arms out in front of her, then turned to Sarah and handed her the cuffs and told her to cuff this stupid ass bitch and very insolent piece of shit slave. Sarah came forward and placed the cuffs firmly around her wrist as Carl brought back two lengths of chain and hung them from the ceiling hooks and raised and attached each of Betty's arms to them as she now looked down. He then stood in front of her very close and held her head up in his left hand and asked her if she had anything to say to her mistress. Betty said she was very sorry mistress Sarah. Carl said he couldn't let her be disrespectful at any time and in any way and above all hitting his wife to be and her mistress and did she understand how this really and truly hurt him inside after all he had done for her as he repeated himself again, she replied she was very sorry again. Carl slapped her, and Betty now knew Carl was going to be extra hard on her now and she was really scared; she looked and felt scared, and began begging for mercy before he even started. Carl said you want mercy, and said I will give you real mercy and asked if she wanted to leave here, right now, he would gladly release her right this minute and pack her bags and take her to a shelter. Betty started crying and pleaded with him no master, no please master, I am very sorry please let me stay. So you know then that Mistress Sarah is going to punish you, and then when she is finished with your tramp ass I am also. He looked at Sarah's face, the side Betty had slapped, it was now red, then at Betty and said you will pay for that. Oh and by the way since you told her if she couldn't punish you she didn't deserve being your mistress, well rest assure I am going to make sure she whips your ass until it bleeds, and you will remember this day as long as you live here bitch, he then spat in her face and slapped her again. He brought back some ankle cuffs and the spreader bar and attached them to Bettys ankles and attached the bar spreading her legs as far apart as possible as she now was fully exposed. He was slow but methodical as he returned to the table and brought back a heavy leather strap along with a whip, he handed the whip to Sarah and had her stand before Betty and asked what she had to say to her mistress. Betty raised her head as tears ran from her eyes and said she was very sorry mistress and deserved to be punished by her. Carl sat at the bar and told Sarah to begin, and the first thing she did was slap Betty again as hard as she could several times, as hard as her small hands would allow. They must have been really hard as Bettys head reeled from the blows as Sarah then spat in her face also, then walked behind her and raised the whip and began Betty's punishment, and then stood in front of her whipping her even more. Sarah stopped only after about twenty minutes as Carl walked over and looked at her, and asked her what you have to say now, tramp ass bitch, she said thank you mistress Sarah. He told her this is for disrespecting my home. As Carl began whipping Betty with another whip, the long wide and much heavier leather whip making it wraparound her quivering body with each blow to her back, ass, thighs, stomach, breast, calf's, and between her legs as he circled her, when he stopped he took the other whip from Sarah and circled her again as she quivered and reeled from the punishment. Carl was really upset with Betty as his strikes weren't light, but had real force behind them like never before. When he stopped he stood in front of her and asked her what you have to say for yourself you stupid ass cunt. She raised her head and said she was very, very sorry, and said, thank you master Carl as tears ran down her face. He slapped her again before reaching between her legs, she was now extremely wet, and then he went to the table and returned with some clamps and placed them on her vaginal lips and one on her clit as she screamed out and howled out in sheer pain. Then he placed some on her now very swollen nipples, he then went and sat by Sarah and asked her to use the heavy leather paddle with the long handle and metal studs on her. Sarah complied and spanked Betty very hard on her ass cheeks, thighs, stomach, and breast as she jerked feeling real pain but unable to move and watching her ass turn red as large whelps slowly began to appear. After twenty or so smacks, Sarah returned and sat down. Carl fixed a drink for them as he allowed Betty to just hang and suffer before he would decide when he would remove the clamps, and what he might do next. He knew that he had to make Betty really suffer this time if he was to maintain control because he had treated her very well and knew she really enjoyed and wanted to be here and especially now with Yan, but also knew she enjoyed being punished, but not like what she was going to endure now and would make damn sure she really suffered this time for sure now. He sat and sipped his drink looking at the helpless and stupid ass Betty hanging with her head down. After half an hour he approached Betty, raised her drooping head and looked into her eyes, they were filled with tears as large red whelps and bruises began to appear all over her shapely body and he cruelly began to slowly twist the clamps before removing them as she winced and moaned and cried feeling real pain before he removed them all as he played with and smacked her now very swollen pussy very hard until she

166

had a violent climax. He blindfolded her and fixed him and Sarah another drink.

They sat and looked at her hanging like a piece of raw meat as Carl said to Sarah don't feel sorry for her, she wanted you and I to punish her this way, that's why she slapped you. Telling Sarah yesterday wasn't enough for her; this was long overdue in her mind and she needed a reason to provoke you and especially me since I brought you here. He told Sarah about what had happened after the first time she had come to dinner and he made Betty stay in her bedroom. Sarah had been very quiet the whole time and said she wanted Carl, he said we have to finish this first. Carl brought the cage over to the center of the basement floor and began releasing Bettys legs and let her hang there as he returned to the bar and sipped some more of his drink, then he removed the blindfold, the cuffs and laid Betty down as she collapsed on the cold floor before making her kneel as he removed the wrist and ankle cuffs, then brought back the shackles and attached them to her arms and legs as he made her stand before making her crawl around the basement as he then continued to whip her with a cruel leather flogger whip that drew some blood from her now much swollen buttocks before placing her in the cage and locking it. Betty looked so helpless with the whip marks and now bruises all over her shapely body, and shackles on in her cage but Carl knew she was happy inside and would release her tomorrow or whenever he felt she was ready. After being caged Betty shortly urinated on herself and would later defecate. Carl was unconcerned knowing she would have to clean it up anyway. He held Sarah and asked if she felt better now, and said much better now that the bitch knows her place and who was in charge.

They finished their drinks and went upstairs as Carl turned off the basement lights and left a distraught, quivering and crying Betty for the night. Carl and Sarah had fun in bed as they made love and showered and climbed back in bed and talked as they kissed. Carl said he was very disappointed that had to happen, but then on the other hand he felt Betty was jealous of her because he had brought her here first. He believed it was her resentment that made her slap and provoke you not because of how you felt after seeing what she had endured. Carl said he felt she was now over it because he had told her he loved her and didn't want to miss treat her and knew she had went too far and stepped over the line. Sarah described how she felt when she looked at the videos of Betty and told Carl she became aroused and had to relieve herself and had never felt that way before. He said it was quite alright and normal and said he had been aroused as he watched also and repulsed at the same time. He and Sarah kissed and he held her and said he loved her and she was a normal human being as they soon went to sleep.

# Ten

The next morning Carl woke up very early way before everyone else, and well before seven am, he cleaned himself up and put on his shorts, a t-shirt and headed downstairs to the basement, turning on the basement lights. Betty was asleep in her cage and was awakened when he entered; there was the faint smell of feces as he took out a small plastic dust pan and bucket from the closet where the mop and bucket were kept. He unlocked the cage where Betty was locked inside, and told her to get out in a cruel and angry voice, she crawled out and told her to clean up her mess as he dropped the bucket and dust pan on the floor before her, she began scooping up her excrement into the bucket and when she had gotten as much up as possible using her hands and the dust pan Carl made her take it to the bathroom and dump it into the toilet, then to stand in the shower as he turned the water on her but kept it on the cool side as she shivered and handed her some soap and a wash cloth. She still had the shackles on; they were plastic as Carl warmed the water very slowly until she almost stopped shivering. He then removed the shackles and had her clean them and herself again then making her get the bucket and a couple rags without letting her dry herself off as he poured disinfectant into the bucket and told her to clean her cage and the floor around it as he watched her very closely. She said nothing as she cleaned it up dumping the bucket several times until Carl was fully satisfied as he folded up her cage and took it into the shower where he made her clean it thoroughly again for a final cleaning. He had her clean the floor on her hands and knees where the cage had been located overnight before he led her back into the shower and made her take a douche and an enema and made her sit on the toilet until he was fully satisfied as Betty now felt fully intimidated, humiliated and very much ashamed. Then made her mop up the basement floor again, turning on the ventilator for the basement to clear the air as he sprayed air freshener, he then attached the leash to her collar, which he had never removed. He then looked into her face holding her head with one hand and slapped her on both sides of her face asking her did she learn her lesson, she said, yes sir master Carl. She began crying as he looked at the whelps, bruises and whip marks. He said to her that he was very sorry she had made the mistake that made him have to resort to becoming like Harold. But unlike Harold he did really love her very much, but as long as she wanted to stay here she would have to do as he and now Sarah told her, but if she ever wanted to leave she was free to do so at any time. If she stayed he hoped what he did he wouldn't never ever have to do to her again and reminded her he wasn't finished with punishing her stupid ass yet. He removed the leash but left the collar in place, told her she was to remain naked the rest of the day but to go rub herself down with some salve and oil and then return to see him in the kitchen and not to wake anyone else since it was before seven in the morning.

Carl remained downstairs in the kitchen and made a pot of coffee while she was away. Betty soon returned and when she did, reported back and stood in front of him, he slapped her again several more times as his coffee was about finished brewing, and told her that yesterday would be a walk in the park if she ever provoked Sarah or him again and above all disrespected him again by her actions, and asked her if she fully understood what he said and meant, she said, yes sir master Carl. He slapped her once again and told her to bend over on one of the kitchen stools. He pulled out a leather belt he had rolled up in his pocket, told her to spread her legs as far apart as possible and he then began whipping her swollen buttocks and between her legs and inner thighs as hard as he could until he was fully satisfied as she now fully understood his anger. Carl didn't know how many times he had struck Betty. Sarah had awoken earlier and found the bed empty and that he was gone and looked around in the bathroom before she started heading downstairs just as he slapped Betty the first time as she stood unseen on the wide stairs as he whipped her even more and had heard every word of what he said to her, as he continued whipping Betty, Sarah cringed as if she could feel every lash herself. When he told Betty to stand, she was in tears and her buttocks was very red and bruised as he then led her to a corner and made her kneel with her hands on her head and stay there until he told her to move. He poured himself a cup of coffee, as he sat and ate a couple donuts. Then he told Betty to stand up and turn around. He asked her if she had anything to say for herself as tears just ran down her pretty face, she said it would never happen again Master Carl and begged him for mercy as she knelt before him and pleaded and said she was very sorry. He told her you will not wear any clothes today, no matter who sees you, or until I say so you stupid ass bitch. He stood in front of her and asked her if she wanted to leave here and be on her own again, she said no please, no master, please Master Carl no I beg of you to let me stay and serve you and mistress Sarah. He said, then you understand your place, she said yes sir master Carl. Betty knew now she had crossed a line she shouldn't have and knew Carl cared for her and even loved her and she had pushed him too far and didn't think he would ever have caused her the physical pain she was now feeling. Told her she was to wait on Sarah all day, hand and foot, you understand and told her to get the harness from the basement, she went and brought it back and he made her go back and get a butt plug also and when she returned he bent her over, stuck the plug roughly up into her rectum then attached the harness sticking the large dildo in her vagina and securing it around her waist and told her she would wear it until he was fully satisfied. She replied yes sir master Carl.

Shortly Yan entered and said good morning Master Carl, and he said good morning Yan. Yan asked if master wanted breakfast and he said yes please, and told Betty to go wash her hands and help Yan as he went to check on Sarah. Yan looked at Betty and almost began to cry as Betty's bruises began to become more vivid and pronounced. Carl noticed Yan reaction and said nothing since he figured it could happen to her also. He returned to his bedroom upstairs and found Sarah washing up and she said I see you have been up early this Sunday morning. Told her he had to have something cleaned up.

She didn't even mention she had heard and also seen him slap and severely whip Betty again. Sarah kissed him and said good morning love, he kissed her back and said the girls were working on breakfast and the coffee was ready. She asked. So you let Betty out of her cage and he said yes, and she will serve you all day, and will have to do whatever you want her to do, and if you want to whip her, and then just go ahead and do it. Sarah said how very wonderful as he locked up the videos and photo album related to Betty. Sarah said she was very sorry and should have listened to him yesterday. He said everyone makes mistakes now and then and said there won't be any more problems with her. Sarah understood what he meant when he said that and didn't have any more questions, and decided to just leave the subject alone.

Carl then went and took a quick shower and put on some clean clothes. Then he and Sarah went downstairs together. Yan had just finished cooking as he and Sarah sat and ate in the kitchen. Yan and Betty ate after they had finished and began to clean up the kitchen. He and Sarah then sat outside on the deck and he drank more coffee and read the Sunday paper. Yan came outside and reported that the kitchen was cleaned up. Sarah suggested he should probably check behind her sometimes. Carl went and checked and found everything was in order. Betty appeared and knelt down and addressed Sarah, mistress, she said, I am her to serve you all day as instructed by Master Carl. Sarah said very well; and kept on reading the paper and talking to Carl after he returned from inside. Carl told Betty to clean the deck and then check the pool and use the skimmer. She went and did as she was instructed as he looked at her whelps, bruises and swollen red buttocks. After an hour Carl called Betty over and removed the harness but left the butt plug in, after removing the harness and dildo from her vagina, made her open her mouth and stuck it in her mouth and made her hold it for several minutes before telling her to go clean it and put it away then return. Sarah said the collar and no clothes is so intimidating that maybe Yan should be wearing hers and stripped for the day since they will be together, if one is disobedient they both will pay the price, because if they like or love each other then they wouldn't want their lover punished. Carl said excellent idea as Sarah left to get Yan. When she returned Yan was nude and had her collar on. Sarah ordered her to help Betty. Carl and Sarah sat and read the newspaper and watched as their two servants cleaned up the deck. Carl ordered Betty and Yan in front of him, told them to kneel as he now informed them that if ever he or Sarah was ever displeased with one, both would be punished and told Yan to take a good hard look at Betty. Yan turned to look at her and immediately began crying, Carl told them to go clean the basement floor again and especially the cage, and let him know when they were finished. They said yes sir and departed to do their assigned task.

Sarah knelt down before Carl after they departed and said watching them made her want to undress and take a swim because it turned her on so much she needed to cool down and regain some of her self-control. Carl said he would get some towels and robes and would be right back. He went inside the house as Sarah undressed and sat at the edge of the pool with her feet in the temped water, and when she saw Carl return she jumped in. He soon joined her as they swam in the buff floating around with an inner tube he had. They kissed having fun and just relaxed. Well over an hour later Yan and Betty appeared and Carl instructed them to vacuum the entire house even the empty bedrooms. After they left he asked Sarah as they sat with robes on what ideas she had for those empty rooms. She said her bedroom furniture in one and didn't know what else. Because she was thinking about her office move more than anything else since it was at the moment the most important thing she was concerned with. Carl said yes that's right and said he was in no rush, but he would have the windows cleaned by the end of the week. He told Sarah he was going to take a nap; the water had relaxed him and he needed some rest. They went upstairs just as Yan finished with his bedroom and he took a quick shower rinsing the pool water out of his hair and off of his skin and applied some lotion before getting in bed followed closely by Sarah after she had also rinsed off. She rubbed him with some oils and he soon fell asleep. The windows were open throughout the house and the mild warm air felt good as they lay down together.

A couple hours later when he awoke and put his shorts on, he walked to Bettys room where he found Yan rubbing salve and oils on Betty's bruised and very tender body, as the whelps and whip marks slowly began to disappear, Yan looked up at him a little frightened, but Carl told her to continue as he turned and walked away. He went back to Sarah who was still lying in bed and climbed in besides her as she woke and rolled over. Carl looked at her as she reached out for him and said she wanted him, Carl hugged and felt on and caressed her as he laid down saying he needed another rub down and she soon began messaging him again, Carl soon dosed off again. When he woke up found he was alone, went and washed his face then went looking in Betty's room and found her and Yan sleeping soundly, both were still naked but had a light blanket over them, he left and rode the elevator downstairs and looked around, then headed to the basement where he found Sarah sitting at the bar having a drink, she looked up when she saw him an ran to him and kissed him, and held him tight, she looked up into his face and said she loved him very much, he kissed her forehead and held her, but he sensed there something was really bothering her, but didn't ask.

She then asked Carl to tie her up and spank her again; she then said please Master Carl and knelt on the floor. He told her to stand up and undress, she did and he returned from the table coming back with a pair of cuffs, she held her arms out before her, he put them on her then brought back a couple lengths of chain, then lifted her arms above her head and attached each to a hanging chain. He held her pretty face in his hands, and she said please whip me, please, make me feel real pain like you made Betty feel this morning please Master Carl, make me yours. He said to her, so you saw me this morning didn't you, she replied yes she had, and had hear every word, and even though it was very harsh and cruel, it turned her on and have been hot thinking about it ever since and her pussy was throbbing inside. Carl turned and walked away before he brought back the ankle cuffs and the spreader bar, attaching them to his future wife before returning to the table. He came back with a ball gag which he attached to her after he kissed her first, and then placed it in her mouth and securing it behind her head. He had the wide strap, he passed it over her lightly and didn't want her anticipating his moves and decided to use the blindfold on her also, covering her eyes, and stood back and just looked at her. He decided to start with a whip, whipping her lightly at first, concentrating on her ass, before he whipped her thighs, breast, stomach, calf's and back then changed and used a cat of nine tails flogger on her, whipping her all over as he began circling her, as he watched her jerk now with each blow. He stopped and let her hang several minutes before removing the blindfold, and gag. He kissed her again as she tonged him back before he again started, this time with the wide leather strap to her thighs, and vagina, ass, and tits. She was now whimpering, then he struck her harder the next several times as she now began jerking violently with each blow, he stopped and stood close to her face, and asked her what was she. She answered she was his dirty slut bitch, as he pinched her nipples and she cringed as he did so, he then began feeling between her thighs and her now very swollen vagina and rubbed it roughly as she quickly came to a rousing climax.

Carl left briefly bringing back a dildo with little soft fingers on it, he poured some oil on it then inserted it in to her quivering pussy and soon she was breathing hard before she exploded again. He then reached over and inserted another penis shaped dildo up her anus and worked the both of them back and forth at the same time as she moaned now having continuing unending climaxes as he whispered she was being fucked like a whore, she then exploded as her entire body jerked with the most violent orgasm she ever experienced. He slowly removed both dildos, letting her hang for several long minutes before releasing her ankle cuffs from the spreader bar, he kissed her as he spanked her quivering ass as she kissed him back wildly before he released her arms from the chains above but leaving the cuffs on and placing her over one of the bar stools and pulling himself out and penetrating her vagina hard from behind as she climaxed multiple times before spreading her now very swollen buttocks and welcoming anus as he penetrated her hard. He then stood in front of her as she sucked him off and coming in her mouth and making her swallow all his semen. When he finished with her, he pulled her up by her hair and asked her, what you say now bitch, she said thank you master Carl. He released her wrist from the cuffs as she cried and he held her and said she loved him so very much, and was his bitch. He led her to the basement shower and bathed her like you would a baby, as she melted in his arms again. He dried her and wrapped her in a large plush towel and all but carried her to his bedroom where he placed her in the bed and massaged her with salves and oils all over, and very soon she was sleeping soundly like a baby.

Carl checked on Yan and Betty, Betty was awake and Yan was sleeping, Betty didn't move as he sat on the side of the bed and pulled the blanket back and looked at her, the whip marks and bruises were slowly going away thanks to Yan but were still very visible. He felt Bettys face, she kissed his hand, he covered her back up and went back to his bedroom, fixed a drink and sat on the large couch and thought about all that had happened this week end, today was Sunday and tomorrow was the holiday, Sarah and Yan would leave and then he would return to his normal routine, it was early evening and everyone had eaten breakfast and even he had napped. He finished his drink took off his shorts and shirt and laid back in bed next to the woman who wanted to be his wife, and evidently his submissive also, he had stopped trying to figure out the female mind set. He had Betty, who had become completely submissive to her husband and accepted over time the fact she was nothing but a slave, then there was Sarah, a smart business woman who now had surrendered herself to him completely, and had asked him to marry her. And she had Yan, another who probably without a choice was Sarah's to do whatever she demanded of her. Anyway he looked at it; he had three women to do whatever he wanted to, or with. Not many men have or would ever be in this position. He took a bottle of massage oil out and rubbed on his beloved Sarah again, looking at the whelps and marks on her smooth skin that he had placed on her. He had no choice but to accept it as her form of surrender to him, and offering of sorts, a truly rare form of love and total submission. He massaged her as she moaned and sleep soundly. He ran his hands through her hair and felt her and kissed her cheek, covering her up. He lay with her a long time and soon she awoke and saw he was there with her and she kissed his hand also as he reached over and rubbed her back. She curled up close to him and began to cry, he applied some more oil to her body and she took his hand and placed it between her thighs and closed them tightly as he felt her warmth and as she held him, she soon climaxed again, he continued to feel her and removed his hand and rubbed her ass cheeks as she buried her head in his chest and then relaxed. She had fallen asleep again. He held her and then shortly she woke again. She was totally exhausted, he decided to order a couple pizzas, he didn't feel like cooking and felt Yan and Betty had also suffered enough. He told Sarah to stay put and went to his desk and pulled out a menu for the nearest pizza restaurant that delivered, he ordered two extra-large deluxe pizzas and they said it would be about an hour. He pulled some cash from his wallet and laid it on his desk, then went and washed his hands.

He checked again on Yan and Betty, they both were awake now, he told them to remove the collars and put on clean some panties and t-shirts and cleanup the kitchen and put everything away. And told them they would be eating soon. They both answered, yes sir, Master Carl as he left going back to Sarah and said he would be back as he took the money and went downstairs. Betty and Yan were straightening things up and told them to put a roll of paper towels on the dining room table. He took out some large picnic plates, told them to take them also as he found some plastic cups. They returned and he handed them to Yan to place on the dining room table as he placed a plastic table cloth on it spreading it out and arranged the table. About fifty minutes later the front doorbell rang and Carl took the money, telling Yan to get Sarah and tell her to come downstairs to eat. He went to the door and paid for the two pizzas and brought them to the dining room table. He told Yan and Betty to sit together after they had washed their hands and Sarah soon appeared in her robe. Carl poured everyone a cup of soda and they all began to eat, he could tell they were all famished.

Everyone ate their fill, there was less than a quarter of a pizza left when they all finished, and Carl asked if they were now satisfied. They said yes and he had Betty and Yan clean up as he placed the remaining pizza in a plastic container and placed it in the refrigerator. Afterwards, he told everyone to go to bed and for Yan and Betty to shower before they did. Yan asked Master Carl if she and Betty could have each other again, he said yes after they showered and oiled one another first. They had until the following morning. He took Sarah to the bedroom after closing the windows and locking up the house downstairs and fixed her a nice strong drink. They sat and talked some more as he held and caressed her before they went to bed.

# Eleven

The following morning when Carl woke after using the bathroom and returned to the bedroom he looked at Sarah, she was still sound asleep. He put on his shorts and shirt and went and checked next on Betty and Yan, they were just waking up. After they had finished washing up, Carl sat on the side of their bed and asked if they had enjoyed their time together. Yan said she now had a friend and lover, and Betty said she loved Yan very much. Carl hugged them both and said he loved them also. Yan started to cry as he held her, he told her everything would be all right and she would always have a home here. He kissed her, and then Yan said, thank you, you are a very nice man and Yan loves you Master Carl. He thanked her then hugged Betty and asked her if she was all right now as he looked at her nude body, she was looking much better as most of the whelps were gone or going away and only some light bruises remained. He told them to clean themselves and then prepare breakfast as he departed. He returned to the bedroom and Sarah was still sleeping, he didn't wake her but went downstairs and put on a pot of coffee and began opening up the windows and letting fresh air flow through the large house. He sat down and had his first cup of coffee as Yan and Betty entered and began preparations for breakfast. He soon returned upstairs just in time to find Sarah just beginning to awaken, she opened her eyes and saw his face and smiled as he sat down on the edge of the bed and began hugging her. Said she loved him so very much and held him tightly as he rubbed her back. She started crying again and said she didn't want to leave, he held her head in one hand and she calmed down as he told her she was a big girl and soon they would see each other every day. Then told her you will be tired of seeing me then. She started laughing and crying at the same time as he just held her and said he loved her very much and wanted her in his life. She finally got herself together as he stood and helped her up and said the girls are waiting on madam to come downstairs for breakfast, she said ok and went to tidy herself up.

They had a beautiful breakfast as usual as Yan and Betty served them, they soon finished eating and went outside and sat on the deck in the morning sun and talked. Carl telling her he would send her all the information on who to call for her new office setup first thing tomorrow, and they will want you to show them what you want done and within a week they will have you all set up and I have another company for your internet service and they will set up a network for you, and also the carpet people. He had worked with them all before and suggested she coordinate them and have them all together at the same time and the work will progress so much faster and they knew what he expected and all she had to do was mention his name, but they also knew where his offices were, and would be very sure she was completely satisfied. He reassured her she would have the information the following day as soon as he reached his office, and if he wasn't in the office when she came by his secretary would have a key for her so she could enter the building anytime she needed to.

He said that he would grill the meats today which he had prepared and had planned to have cook yesterday before the abrupt change of plans. Said he would give them some food to take home with them. Carl checked the grill then went inside and pulled out the pan of meats he had intended to cook yesterday. Betty and Yan went to straighten and clean up and Carl knew where they were. He checked and they had plenty of food and wouldn't have to do anything but grill the meats. He returned to the deck and added a few more coals to the grill and lite it, coming back and sitting next to Sarah. She told him how exciting the weekend had been and was extra happy especially now because she had reached a new level of sexual release now and really felt freer now than she ever had before. Told him how much he meant to her and how much she loved him. Carl checked the grill and retrieved the pan of meats and returned and placed it on the side table, then again sat next to Sarah. She again said it had been the most enjoyable weekend ever and looked forward to many, many more together.

Carl soon began cooking, running inside right quick and bringing back some buns, after grilling a few brats, handed Sarah one, as they ate one hot and fresh off the grill. They ate the brats and Sarah said that was oh so good as Carl returned to cooking, he had several chicken breast, brats and Italian sausage, and some hamburger patties and it wasn't very long before he was soon finished since he had  closely watched his meats cooking, making sure they cooked evenly and weren't overdone. When he finished, he brushed the grill with his grill brush and closed it to smother the fire. He returned to the kitchen with the meats and covered them up. He returned to the deck where Sarah was sitting and enjoying the pleasant weather and suggested they go upstairs and he would help her pack before going home. Carl said we can always eat later, they went upstairs and Sarah asked him to make love to her, she undressed and they lay in the bed as he held her close and they felt on one another and soon were engaged again in some hot steamy sex, and after having multiple organisms Sarah rolled over exhausted again. Carl looked at her and held her in his arms, she began to cry again and said she really didn't want to leave him, but he comforted her by telling her, I will see you almost every day very soon so don't fret baby girl, it will all work out very soon. They showered one last time together and had more sex in the shower as Carl took full advantage of her and they finally emerged to lie in the bed and massaged one another. They eventually after a long and sensual petting session put their clothes back on as Sarah began packing her clothing and Carl left to find Yan. He soon found her and instructed her to begin packing her suitcase also, and when he did he find her, both her and Betty were sitting and talking, and holding hands in Betty's large bedroom. Carl told Yan to pack as he returned to Sarah.

Sarah and Yan took their suitcases downstairs as they prepare to have their last weekend meal together with Carl and Betty. Betty and Yan set the table for four as instructed by Carl in the dining room. Soon they were all sitting at the same table and enjoying a great meal of the salads and grilled meats while Carl poured wine for all. He proposed a toast to our new family. Everyone was fully satisfied. They finish eating and Betty and Yan cleaned up the dining room and kitchen as Sarah and Carl sat in the living room holding one another. He told Sarah to call when she got home and then he could rest knowing she was home safe. He reassured her that it won't be very long before they will all be under one roof, and telling her he will see her very soon during the coming week probably at work and maybe tomorrow or the following day for sure, and anyway she will always be on his mind and especially in his heart. It was getting late when Yan and Betty said everything was cleaned up, and Sarah said it was time for them to depart. Carl said he would give them some food to take if they wanted and Sarah said she sure would appreciate it. He then fixed them a couple of carry home containers and placed it all in a polyethylene shopping bag.

He and Sarah kissed as he walked her and Yan to the garage, Yan and Betty hugged and kissed one another, and Yan got into Sarah's car and they pulled out of the garage and departed down the long driveway heading toward home. Betty had tears in her eyes as Carl asked her, what was bothering her. She said that she would miss Yan very much. He and Betty went back inside and Betty turned to Carl and asked him what he wanted her to do and he said tidy up and to change all the sheets and make up the beds, she said, yes sir master Carl, and departed to do her duties. Carl went downstairs too shot some pool and fixed a drink and shortly Sarah called, saying they were home safe. He told her he loved her and soon they would see each other, they hung up, and afterwards he finished his drink and checked and locked up the house and went upstairs and thought about going to bed early after checking that Betty had changed his sheets and her own. Betty was taking her shower and finished just as he entered her room, and after she dried off he rubbed her down with some salve and massage oils as he looked at the remaining marks which were almost gone. When he finished she kissed him and he hugged her, said she was very sorry she had made him so very angry at her and said it would never ever happen again and she loved him very much, he kissed her and said to her, get some sleep.

It was still a little early as Carl looked at the clock and something kept nagging him about those last videos Harold had made and his reference to the end is near, and taking out the trash or something on that order. Carl kept thinking since he seemed to have picked up on Harold's way of doing things, felt there was something he either over looked or missed and decided he had some time now to look and decided to see if there was more, maybe something, somewhere as he reached under his large desk and pulled out the camera cases that belonged to Harold, and the laptop he had brought here along with Betty, it had been several months now since that fateful day when he brought Betty home with him and always wondered about fate or some unforeseen reason why she was placed in his life as he was just getting around to seeing what else there might be he missed especially after the events of this past weekend. He opened up the laptop only for about the third time since he had it in his possession and turned it on and while waiting for it to boot up he opened up the video camera case. This might be the answer he was looking for. With just a laptop Carl had always wondered how Harold had created so many DVD disc without having a PC or a recording program even though all of the disc were recorded in data or mp4. The camera recorded directly to the disc. After opening the case found a small container that held the blank unused disc, the camera itself, power cord, extra battery, operator's manual and charger. It was one very nice compact setup. He opened the camera and found a disc inside and also one inside a paper sleeve labeled completed and wondered if there was anything recorded on it. He took the one in the paper sleeve out first as he entered the password into the laptop, and that was Ronald. How poetic he thought, the dead baby's name since Harold had listed all his information on the index card and Carl had kept everything together as he again looked at the screen saver of Betty in her cage crying, and remembered it was also one of the photos Harold had uploaded to the internet bondage site. He placed the disc from the paper sleeve into the tray and pushed it in, waited for it to spin up and then hit the play icon, to his surprise it was Harold again as he sat and began talking into the camera and then he momentarily stopped, and panned to a wider angle and again it was mounted on the tripod. Harold began speaking and started over again from the beginning as Carl wondered if he had any idea this would be one of his last video conversations as he looked at the date and it was from six days before his untimely death. Carl now looked and listened intently as Harold began with a wide shot of the apartment and Betty completely nude in her cage and it appeared she was asleep. Harold did a close up and made some derogatory comments about her and stated he had just drugged her stupid ass and was seeing how easily he could drug her this time he was using cough syrup and it seemed to be pretty effective for what he wanted to do to her as he planned her demise. Said he was going to the store shortly and buy his favorite beer and begin his planned weeklong celebration and it would culminate with Betty's demise as he began laughing and that particular session ended. The next seen was as Harold then mounted the camera on the tripod and explained he was really tired of Betty, and was in the next very few days was going to finally dispose of her and it would be in remembrance of Ronald's tenth birthday if he had lived and soon in celebration of his death he was going to dispose of the shit in his life soon after the next upcoming holiday weekend. He said he was going to take advantage of moving to a warmer climate and possibly collecting on some old insurance policies and his job had another warehouse operation located in Florida and he was going to transfer and it had just come through and he was moving as soon as the lease here ran out since he was only taking his clothes. He said it was time Betty had a fatal accident and then he could collect the insurance moneys from her demise and was making this as his personal record for his own private collection. Said he hated her so fucking much and was thinking about torturing her maybe with some hot irons or maybe saying she had been kidnapped and tortured and killed by a wild rapist or somebody really crazy as he busted out laughing, but said she didn't have long to live and was going to really hurt her over the next following weeks before he disposed of her since she had no family she wouldn't be missed since she was trash anyway. Said he had found a nice place to hide her body and she would never be found, as he continued laughing about it. Said he was thirsty and maybe would record some more thoughts later and that session ended. It started again as Harold said he was tired of her period and it was time he started over again as he went on to describe the different ways he thought of disposing of Betty, and went on to say even if he didn't collect on the insurance her time was up anyway. Harold went on to say he was thinking of burying her alive by putting her drugged ass in a wooden box, covering it with dirt and just leaving and had found the ideal location no one would find, at least while she was alive. He also thought of throwing her off a bridge onto the interstate making it look like a suicide or making her do it or even better burning her alive here in the apartment, but preferred to do it elsewhere as she would die from or suffocate from smoke inhalation or be incinerated. Carl was in total shock, but then again the way he treated her it was no surprise, then he thought about the unfinished letter addressed but undated for the apartment complex management that said he wasn't going to renew the lease. The next scene was Harold was somewhere out in the country as he explained there was a farm on one side of the dirt road he was standing on as he stood and took pictures of the location and explained the forest preserve was on the other side along with a portion of the backside of Honey Woods Cemetery, and this was where all the property lines came together as he took good pictures of the location. He went on to show a steel drum without a top more than half way buried in the ground near a deep drainage ditch and said he had just decided to burn Betty alive today and she was in the car waiting. Said he wanted to torture her one last time and make her feel his pain and thought this would be the perfect location and the way of disposing the shit in his life and would just cash in the insurance policies on her soon to be dead ass. A few minutes passed as Harold explained as he set the camera on the tri pod several yards further away with a wide angle view of the car and the location of the barrel, and you could see the corn field and the corn was only a couple feet tall which meant it was far from mature, so this was in early spring. He walked over and opened the car door and told Betty to get out, she climbed out and stood looking at Harold with a really frightened look on her face as he commanded her to crawl which she did as he fastened the leash to her collar and then made her kneel as he said take a good look bitch, and pointed to the barrel. He then made her stand as she was wearing just a short skirt and blouse, as he then made her climb into the half buried barrel only after he tore the blouse open and almost completely off exposed her breast and then snatched the thin worn skirt off as it ripped and fell around her ankles. After she had climbed down inside the barrel, he tied her hands behind her back, she appeared drugged but conscious as he then said he made her drink half a bottle of cough syrup, he then removed a five gallon metal gas can from the trunk of the car. He screamed at her as he knelt down in front of her and told her today you die you stupid ass bitch as he slapped her one last time and laughed, then spat in her face and pointed and told her to look at the camera as she turned and looked. Harold was walking toward the gas can and was only a few minutes away from pouring the gasoline over her when, just as Harold reached the can you could hear the low drone of an approaching airplane, then as it became louder, seemingly out of nowhere a crop duster airplane appeared passing very low, not even twenty feet overhead spraying and covering the edge of the corn field and then returned again as he made another pass back over the corn field going the other way and continued.

Harold now suddenly panicked as he quickly put the gas can back inside the open car trunk instead of walking to where Betty was, and went and roughly pulled Betty out of the barrel and dragged her back to the car as he roughly pushed her inside the back seat with her hands still tied now completely naked, then ran back and grabbed the camera never turning it off and tossing it inside the back as it was laying on the floor still recording, you could hear him cuss as he quickly departed and you could hear the crop-duster as the lens was now pointed upward and partially see Betty as she eventually rolled on top of the camera as Harold made a quick exit from the location. The plane continued down the rows of corn, the camera stopped recording while Harold was still driving down the bumpy back road only the farmer used. The next disc was still inside the camera and was of Harold again as he explained he was going to send Betty on a one-way mission she would never return from. And said he was just sorry burning her didn't work out as planned but had no intentions of getting caught killing her, and knew the pilot had a good view of the ground. Said he was very sorry that didn't work out because he really planned on putting part of that one on the internet, and had imagined watching her burn as she screamed. He now explained he was going to send her to the twenty-four hour grocery store about a mile away when it was just getting dark and on her way back home it would be when she would get killed, he was going to hide in a wooded area she had to pass by and make it appear she was raped and murdered, then he could collect on the insurance money and was planning to do it very soon, like tomorrow evening and said he would take pictures and was all prepared as he photographed Betty eating out of the dog bowls with her hands tied behind her back with a anal plug inside of her and Harold said take a good look at the dog ass bitch as she has her last supper. Harold went on as the camera was on Betty that she would be well seen as she passed through the neighborhood since he had made her walk to the store before and return with a couple of heavy bags and had observed people looking at her and heard their remarks about her shabby dress and poor appearance when she was out in public. And several times being harassed and made fun of by teenagers as she was forced to walk as he observed from his car and it wouldn't be unusual if the police came and interviewed him about her disappearance and especially when they found her body. Said he had it all planned out and maybe it would just happen by accident, but anyway tomorrow was the big day, little Ronald's birthday. What a bastard Carl thought, that recording was made just the day before his fatal accident, how God worked in such mysterious ways since he was killed in a one car accident and no one else was injured, hurt or even involved.

Carl started crying again, held his head in his hands and prayed a long time; he thanked God that he had allowed Betty to be here with him and said she was safe. He stood and walked to Betty's room, he knocked this time before entering and found her sleeping peacefully as he sat on the edge of the bed and she awoke looking up at him and smiled, she sat up after she saw the tears in his eyes and hugged him as he hugged her tightly and told her she was safe here with him and Sarah. He was too choked up to tell her now why he was here except he wanted to be sure she was safe, he kissed and held her and soon returned to his bedroom. Betty was scared now and didn't know what to do, but stayed in her bedroom and finally was able to go back to sleep. Carl returned and fixed himself a drink, and then he scanned through all the laptops documents and opened every file and scanned every photo before he shut it down making sure he didn't miss anything. He left it out and plugged up and would think about what he should do as far as revealing what he knew but would first ask Betty if she remembered the incident. He would have to see if telling Sarah if Betty remembered was worth the anguish and sorrow it might bring on. One thing for sure he was going to have a couple of stiff drinks now before climbing into bed.

# Twelve

The following day when Carl entered his office and turned on his computer, the first thing he did was gather all the information he needed to send Sarah. After several minutes he had it all organized and began typing it out after gathering all the needed information, he then sent Sarah and e-mail with all the information that she would need for the office equipment, carpet and internet installers, and was able to offer her several different choices, but with his preferred choices first, as he grouped them together as exceptional, best and then better, and went a step further by numbering them also, with little side notes. Then he sent her a text telling her to check her e-mail, and that he loved her very much and missed her already. He then proceeded to check his own business and had brief conversations with both John and Mary and told them both about his engagement to Ms. Sarah Rogers and she would be the new tenant upstairs very soon then after clearing his e-mail accounts and walking around as he usually did checking the building and then his service and construction crews greeting everyone personally before they departed for jobs and calls and returned to his office. He started by and reading the daily newspapers and the foreclosure and sheriffs sales in the classified section before checking property listings on the RELS around the immediate area. He informed his secretary Pat about a set of keys for Sarah if she decided to pick them up and said Mary would have them and for her to see Mary if she came in and asked about them. She might pick them up before the work was completed or if she needed access to the building after hours and told her she was the new tenant for the upstairs office space. He soon departed as he headed to some nearby property locations and checking out a strip mall property that was soon coming up for auction and didn't return until a little after twelve noon. His secretary informed him that an extremely attractive woman, a Ms. Rogers had stopped by and asked for him and said she didn't need the keys yet as she waited on a couple gentlemen from an office furniture supplier and communication companies to meet her before they all went upstairs together. Carl said very good, as he returned to his office and called his building maintenance department and soon one of his men appeared at his office door and he told them about having several reserved parking spots added next to his and gave him a sheet of what to print on the signs and how he wanted the first row at the entrance arraigned and informed him to have the windows cleaned inside and out doing upstairs first. Carl thanked him as he departed. It was midafternoon around two pm and decided to call it a day and soon headed for home.

Sarah also had a very busy day as she called her staff together and informed them of the up and coming move and gave them the new address, and said pack up everything that wasn't necessary to keep the office functioning for the next couple of weeks and also had her number two handle the office as she left to meet with the internet and office furniture supply people. As she was giving great thought and thinking about how she wanted her new office configured as she remembered how the

large space looked after calling the office supply people
and making an appointment to meet them at the new
location and if possible all of them together today at ten
this morning. She had also called the people who would
set up the internet and telephone service for her. After
telling them she would be there with the office supply
people and where it was located and giving them the
building address. Oh they said Mr. Hogan's building and
stated they would try and come at the same time, she
thanked them and called the carpet people and gave them
the same time to meet her at the new location also if
possible. She opened her office at eight and would meet
them at ten, and soon left out after informing Carol Gene,
her second in command to take over while she was gone
and soon arriving at her new office location and checking
in with Carl's secretary Mary Sue. Mary Sue was very
attractive, fifty six and widowed, five nine and about one
hundred fifty pounds, brunette, with a very pretty face
and real nice figure; she was very efficient and was in
charge of the small staff that consisted of several other
women who handled the office. Sarah was very surprised
at how well managed, and efficient after a young woman
greeted her as she made her request. Shortly after
entering she was asked to follow and she was led to Mary
Sue Anderson's lavish office and spoke with Mrs.
Anderson as she stood and they greeted one another and
Mary Sue welcomed her and said she was happy that he
had found someone for the space upstairs and she also
congratulated her on her up and coming marriage to Carl.
Sarah thanked her as Mary Sue handed her a key and
Sarah said she would rather get it a little bit later but was

hoping Carl was in. Mary said good luck on that one sister, since he was in and out frequently and said the early morning was the best time to catch him. Mary walked with her back to the hallway and said it was a pleasure and was glad Carl had found a beautiful and intelligent woman to be his wife and wished her all the happiness in the world, Sarah held out her hand to shake and Mary took it and pulled her close and hugged her and said I hope you will be happy here and in life sweetheart. Sarah smiled and said thank you very much, you make me feel so welcomed. Sarah turned and walked toward the elevator as Mary Sue watched her momentarily before returning to her office.

Sarah found Carl's office to be a real surprise but should have expected as much given his orderly nature and clean habits which she also fell in love with after getting to know him. It was very well managed, extremely efficient, clean and very modern and up to date with each of his clerical staff handling several things and with overlapping duties in case someone was sick or off for some reason. Carl was only there half the time anyway, because he maintained hands on operation and liked to be out surveying and looking for new business opportunities. Besides he had three large apartment complexes and two smaller ones that he owned and frequently checked on personally. He had bought each and completely rehabbed them before renting them out again and did so under different company names and having one woman handle most of all the business associated with their operations and supervising the leasing agents who stayed on each of the premises.

Sarah was fortunate to meet all the representatives of the different companies who would set up her new office at the same time, and all she had to do was choose an office lay out, and they quickly presented her with several different choices after she showed them where she wanted her own office to be located. They began showing and suggesting several different layouts and styles and saying as soon as she chose one she really liked they would take it from there, and gave her an approximate cost. She wanted her personal office where she could see the parking lot and decided on having twin isles parallel with the windows and atrium and cubicles on both sides of one aisle near the center and a single row by the atrium then they would loop around at the end where her office would be located bordering the windows. Her office would be at the far end with two others for the new management positions she would soon create in her operations as she was preparing to institute some new and drastic changes for her offices management by creating teams. She also wanted her office to be large enough to have a small comfortable lounge area with a couple large chairs and possibly a couch where she could speak with prospective clients. Toward the rear near the washrooms would be a conference room for meeting with her employees and also working with clients, and have an area for maybe some lockers or a coat room combination employee lounge. When finished it would be very comfortable, efficient and ultra-modern, she liked the space and especially the open views and sun light. The furniture company representatives said they would coordinate their efforts and work together and give her a cost estimate by early this evening, she thanked them as they all soon departed after measuring the space and checking the internet and phone and power connections. She was happy that she had at least started the ball rolling and couldn't wait to move in especially when she returned to her current very cramped and depressing office space. She would inform the landlord once she had a completion date for the new space, and knew it would cost her several thousand dollars up front, but she could well afford it, and besides it was time to really improve her business situation and the new location would allow her to bring in even more clients and would greatly help in expanding her business operations and make much better and needed efficiencies and also much happier employees, beside it would be a better and more professional atmosphere for everyone involved. She had a very good reputation in her field and tried not to turn down any work because of her cramped office conditions but it was becoming very difficult and it was one of the reasons for her badly needed and very much overdue expansion. That evening about a half hour before she would be heading home, she received, and had a conference call with the three companies involved for the change of location and the rough estimated cost was around eleven thousand and the final cost they projected to be around maybe thirteen thousand dollars at most. She said that was fine and to proceed. They would see her tomorrow morning with the contracts to sign and a preliminary layout for her approval. Very well she replied and said I'm looking forward to the meeting, and they would all meet her here, and then the work would start immediately. They said no more than two weeks at the most until final completion, she thanked them and the call ended.

Sarah knew the initial setup would cost her some serious dollars, but she could well afford it and in the long run it would truly enhance her business and especially her income. It also would provide everyone with a much more pleasant and comfortable atmosphere for her very loyal and trusted employees and really looked forward to the move. She thought about how pleasant it would be to be near her lover and future husband and the rent he was going to charge her was going to be a tremendous savings for her also, and couldn't ask for more. Carl wouldn't be far away and she could see him every day. She sat and thought about how enjoyable her weekend had been with him and how she had finally released all she had been holding inside for so long and how she really felt so free now. Knew she had deep feelings and compassion, but also how she was able to release her anger and not allow it to eat on her. How her punishment of Betty proved she was strong and then how she had surrendered herself to Carl, and given herself to him, and his acceptance of her heart and soul. She was awakened from her thoughts as her last employee was leaving and said good night to her and then she began preparing to leave for home herself.

Such a productive day she thought as she drove home and would relax and have dinner. The following day shortly after opening her office and with only a couple of her employees present, the company representatives came in, she greeted them all as she looked closely at the new layout, agreeing to the new plans and only suggesting some minor changes which would really bring her office from the stone age to the jet age. She would also have the new vertical roller file cabinets, four each would be installed at one central location in the office near the conference room in back which would sort of act as a room divider with space for more if needed, and they took up much less space than the older single vertical file cabinets and there capacity was in the thousands in file capacity and would give her more space to expand if she had to. The office would span the width and length of the large space and have room for more cubes if she decided to or needed to add any more. With the new space she would have a view of the parking lot area and it would be a bright and sunny space as would be the entire office and would have its own Wi-Fi and VPN network and be easily expandable, all she had to do was chose the type of carpet and color, she chose a Berber in a warm green color and a dark green for her office. She signed all the contracts and was reassured that completion would be very timely. The office supply people would give her credit for her old desk, file cabinets and chairs since she was purchasing all new furnishings and would pick them up once she had moved all her files. She called her landlord and informed them she would be gone by the end of the month. He wished her good luck, when she finished her call, she called the moving company that Carl had recommended and they said they would send a person by to give her an estimate that same day. She had completed what she needed to do, and felt better already.

She poured herself a cup of coffee and returned to her desk.

By the time the short four day work week had almost ended, Sarah was totally exhausted from her preparations for the coming move and packing when she received a phone call asking her to come to the new location to finalize the layout before the installers began with the final assembly and installations, they asked her to come Saturday morning as they would be working over the weekend because as one man explained, this was Mr. Hogan's building and he didn't play around, but was very thorough and had provided them with quite a few very large and very profitable jobs and he always insisted on quality. She asked what time and was told eight am would be perfect. That Saturday when she arrived at the new office location, she was surprised to find Carl there also, they hugged and kissed and the representative had ten men waiting. She saw that the internet cables and phone lines had been installed along with the file cabinets and the cubes were out lined with tape on the floor. She looked and walked around the area and said it was what she wanted and they began the assembly right away. The carpet was in place and there were boxes of desk components and on the other unused side were boxes containing her new computers and electronics. She thanked the men and soon her and Carl departed. She asked him what he was doing here and he said his building maintenance department had contacted him and were going to lock up after they finished upstairs today and said usually the offices are closed except for about four hours sometimes, and only one person might be here if at all. He told her he was going to look at a nearby property and then another location where he might bid on a job for some major renovation work. He told her no job was too small for him to look at. He kissed her and said he had to go but would call her later. Sarah had spoken to him several times during the week and wanted to spend some time with him, and he said very soon my dear.

Sarah watched him drive away and then turned and looked up at where her office would be and now felt so much better. She did some grocery shopping before she returned home to relax and get some needed rest while Yan took the grocery bags and put the food away. Later Carl called and said he was on his way home and asked if he could stop by, she said he didn't have to ask and she would be waiting for him. She really missed him so very much and became very excited after his call and began feeling on herself, she never felt like this before about a man and definitely never loved anyone like she loved him. It wasn't long before the doorbell rang and Yan answered the door and said she was upstairs, he took off his shoes as she came downstairs and flew into his arms and hugged him long and hard kissing him all over. They sat on the sofa and discussed her office move. She thanked him for his recommendations and said the people were more competent than she ever expected, said it was hassle free but very tiring for her. Said he would let her get some needed rest since it had been such a short week because of the past holiday weekend and said he wanted to relax also. He told her he missed her and Yan and soon they would discuss their personal plans. He stood and hugged her and said he loved her as he headed for the door. Said she wanted him to stay but understood he needed some rest also. But she asked him to feel on her. Carl hugged and kissed her placing a hand between her warm thighs and whispering dirty words in her ear and she shortly erupted with a massive organism. He held her until she calmed down kissing and biting her before he released her and said he would call later, she cried and said ok love as he slipped on his shoes, kissed her again and departed.

Later that evening Carl called her and Yan answered the house phone and said mistress was asleep and would tell her that he called, and then told her not to wake her. He asked Yan how she was doing and she said very good master Carl, he said good bye and hung up. Betty knocked on his door and asked him when he wanted to eat. He told her later but if she was hungry to go ahead and fix herself something. She said thank you master, and asked if she could play with herself, he told her to come here and had her undress and get in bed with him as he undressed and held Betty, kissing her as he inspected her body as the whelps and bruises had now disappeared, he felt on her as she now became highly excited since Carl had never invited her into his bed. She began trembling tremendous anticipation as he spread her legs open and massaged her very large and highly aroused clitoris as she became very moist as Carl played with her nipples pulling and twisting them knowing how Betty enjoyed the four plays as he stuck his fingers deep inside of her. She soon climaxed and then having her suck them before he climbed on top of her entering her with his large and very hard penis. He rammed her hard after slowly entering her and talked to her in a degrading manner as Betty just continued climaxing multiple times before having her turn over and with her ass up and continuing to having his way with her vagina as she continued climaxing as he spanked her ass hard before entering her anus and pumping it hard and playing with her clit before releasing his pent-up load inside of her, this was the first time he had sex with Betty other than oral and it was a very pleasurable experience. She climaxed several more times and then led her to the bathroom where he gave her a golden shower before they bathed one another and he played with her some more causing her to climax again several more times, she dried him off then herself. Having her to massage him and then he did her. He made her lay besides him as he felt on her again and she was still very highly aroused since he had never done this before with her, she climaxed again as he spanked her vagina and told her she was his slave bitch which excited her even more causing her to climax repeatedly before he stopped. He asked her if she still wanted to play with herself, she said no sir master Carl. He told her to go to her bedroom and take a nap and he would come get her later when he was hungry, as she left he rolled over and went to sleep. About three hours later, it was around seven pm when he woke and found a text message from Sarah, it said you are probably sleeping by now but please call when you wake. He washed his face, put on his shorts and called Sarah. She answered promptly and asked if he slept well and said he had, said she missed him as he told her he had just woke up and was going to get something to eat, then have a drink and sit up a little while before going back to bed.

Sarah told him again how much she missed him. Carl said it won't be very long before they would be together; because times like this, she wanted to be in his arms, he told her he felt the same way. He said he would call her tomorrow, she said good night my love, and he told her he loved her and hung the phone up. He opened Bettys door and found her sleeping as he woke her, and told her they were going downstairs to eat, as he turn to leave she said master Carl. He turned back around, she stood and came and hugged him, kissing him and said she loved him so very much, he held her nude body in his arms and was aroused again by her and told her to put on her shirt and panties as they were now going to eat. She went and freshened herself as he took the elevator downstairs. He took some food he had cooked before out of the refrigerator and began heating it and not long after he and Betty were sitting down together eating. They soon finished and she cleaned up and he told her to come downstairs after she finished and when she did he had fixed a drink for her, they sat and talked. She told him she wanted to serve him more now than ever before and wanted to serve Sarah also, that was her job and it made her so excited thinking about Sarah and would be glad when she returned. He told her he was happy she felt that way because it would be so much better for her. Said she really missed Yan very much and was thankful for her care and compassion when she was here. She made her feel so much better after her punishment. Carl fixed her another drink a little stronger than the last as Betty became even more relaxed and more talkative as she began expressing her true feelings as tears came to eyes and said she was sorry she slapped Sarah and knew she loved her. Carl took a chance and asked her about Harold and just before he had his accident, did she notice any changes in his attitude or actions in the weeks or months before it happened. Betty was even more talkative now and much more relaxed since he had made love to her and felt she knew her place with both him and Sarah. She said he seemed to become more cruel and threatening to burn her with the iron or heat up a coat hanger and brand her and had even drugged her a couple times which was something new and he seemed to see how long she was knocked out and remembered once it lasted two days and then he started only feeding her every other day and kept repeating that she didn't have very long but didn't know what he meant by it until he actually one day said she didn't have long to live, he was drunk and she was locked in her cage. He asked her did she ever remember being in a corn field and having been inside of a steel barrel. She remembered being outside once and Harold stripped her and made her get in a barrel as he yelled at her and made her look into the camera as an airplane flew overhead and Harold suddenly putting her back in the car and then falling asleep. They had another drink and Carl came around the bar and hugged and kissed her, he said there was a reason she was here, and why Harold hit that tree and she might not accept it but he felt God had intervened on her behave and he needed to tell her as he sat down and held her hand and kissed it. He told her the other evening when he came into her room and said he

208

wondered if she was all right. She said it's when you had tears in your eyes, and had been crying said she could tell. Carl went on to tell her it was because he found out that Harold was planning to move out of town, but you weren't going with him, but he was going to murder you for the insurance money and move to Florida and that was the reason why he had the new set of suitcases. Betty looked at him and began crying profusely as she reached out and held Carl as her whole body began to shake and tremble violently as she began to perspire while chills ran through her. Betty shook as she looked up at Carl and said thank you master Carl, thank you for being in my worthless life. Carl held her until she stopped shaking and petted her and said it wasn't worthless, Harold had just made you feel that way, and I am going to help you realize just how very precious and special you are to me and Sarah. When she finally finished crying he cleaned up the bar and secured the house and took and put Betty in her bed, told her she was much loved and needed, kissed her and departed and returned to his bedroom, undressed an took a short shower and soon climbed into bed and went to sleep.

The following morning he woke early, used the bathroom and climbed back in bed and just laid there eventually falling back to sleep. About an hour or so later he woke, went and took a shower, put on some clean clothes and went downstairs. Betty was up and had made the coffee. She fixed breakfast, they ate then she cleaned up and went about her duties. Carl took Harold's laptop and went through the video files again and looked to see if there were any files that weren't on any disk and ran across a couple, some of the last ones since they were by date he had made. Betty was tied to a crude x frame in the living room made of scrap lumber, she was it appeared unconscious as Harold had pumped her nipples into the plastic tubes one inch long as he explained he was still making his freak bitch as he tied the end of her nipples after they came out the other end of the tube before he did the same to her clitoris, using a tube with a larger diameter and was also about two inches long and tied it off also. He then took photos after he placed a mask on her unconscious face and then wrote on her using a lipstick. He wrote whore, bitch and several other derogatory words and then after more than an hour untied her nipples and clit as he removed the tubes. Betty had been drugged as he untied her and laid her on the floor. He took the x frame apart and laid it by a wall before returning and placing Bettys limp body across the cocktail table as he took more photos. This was a month before his accident as he looked into the camera and gave the thumbs up sign, the video ended. Carl said to himself strange as he opened the last file. Evidently, Harold plugged the camera into the laptop as he explained what he was planning to do as he outlined his plan, he had tested a couple different drugs on Betty to see the effect and had a location picked out, he had a large wooden box he was going to place her in, it would be about three to four feet in the ground and he would place her inside alive but drugged, then he was going to cover it with dirt since he hated her and figure it would be his last act of revenge before he started a new life free of her parasitic ass. Carl, after the last video from the camera wasn't as upset this time and especially since he had told Betty of Harold's plan of revenge. Carl unplugged the laptop, shut it down and took it and Harold's camera to his large closet and placed it all on its own shelf.

The rest of the day was uneventful and later he and Betty ate dinner together, she sensed something was on his mind and didn't speak as she remembered the conversation from the day before and knew Carl was very sensitive as he thanked her for cleaning up and returned to his bedroom. He spoke to Sarah a couple times that day. That evening before going to bed Betty asked if she could sleep with him, he asked her why, she said a slave is supposed to comfort her master. He told her to go to her bedroom, which she did without hesitation. Carl after taking a shower laid in bed and thought about women, he had a feeling it was Betty that saw Sarah not so much as her mistress, but as a rival for his attention and thought maybe he and Sarah should switch Yan and Betty around, or that might not be such a good idea, he would have to think about it more as he thought about Harold's plan to bury Betty alive and the terror she would feel if she woke up, what a real bastard he was  and turned over and soon went to sleep.

# Thirteen

The following week turned out to be a happy and wonderful time for Sarah. That Tuesday morning, she checked on her new office with the contractors as the work progressed. She had them install more than twenty cubicle areas, even though she only had eleven employees, the new computers were installed for all her current employees and technicians were installing the server for her and updating all the work stations to include the empty cubicles. The office supply people were putting together the chairs, and the file cabinets were installed an operational. She also had a new and much larger desk, it really was an office suit, one every company president should have, the phones were installed an operational along with the internet, and on Thursday the movers were going to load up her office files and move them here. There was a nice counter with a wet sink outside and behind the large twin washrooms with a very large coffee urn that had been provided as a thank you gift from the office supply company. The technicians who set up her internet were going to be their on Thursday and Friday to help transfer all of her computerized records to the newer machines which would be up and running by the end of the day. She informed her employees, that they would be working Saturday so the following week everything and everybody would start smoothly on Monday morning and they could start at their regular time.

By the close of business Wednesday her office was completely packed up and ready to go, and on Thursday morning the movers took all her files. She checked there weren't any documents or papers left behind. Then the office supply people came and removed all of the old office furniture. The office was completely empty now. Susan called the landlord and he quickly came by as she turned over the keys and he signed a release and said they would mail her deposit check to her new office address. She turned around and never looked back. On Thursday and Friday her employees had spent all day getting settled and organized in her new space and her employees loved the new location, with the sun light and openness and especially with the ample parking. They unpacked and liked the new file cabinets as they set up their own personal cubes and organized the new office. Carl had reserved a space next to his and the entire front row was now marked with several reserved parking spots and the rest was for visitors.

On Saturday, along with her small staff caught up on their work that the move had disrupted and it wasn't long before they had everything arraigned and were soon caught up and finished early because of the new set up and new work stations allowed they to work quicker and more efficiently. They all left at three o'clock when she decided to call it a day. Sarah went home dog ass tired, showered, ate a light meal and went directly to bed. Carl had seen her almost every day that week. She had now prepared her office and was getting things organized and everything was the way she wanted. Carl said that he would be here for her, and not to worry, it would be worth all the added extra effort, because he knew from experience. Carl did call and talked to Yan checking on her but letting her catch up on her long overdue and much needed rest.

It took Sarah no time to adjust to her new surroundings at work and was very glad now she had moved here. She could sit at her desk and see Carl as he came and went during the week. Her hours were eight to five, sometimes six with Saturdays and Sundays off for her and her staff, and soon her office became even more efficient as her business began to soon pick up. After moving she received a short term contract from a major national company to audit the books of one of their local manufacturing subdivisions. She was able to provide them with daily account tracking. They were so impressed that after the contract had run its course and she had stopped working for them they considered hiring her again. Soon after there was a shakeup at the parent company, they called her back and asked if she would accept a long term contract for the entire company. She was surprised since this company had over a billion dollars a year in earnings. She said yes, but would have to go to New York for an interview since they were looking at several different accounting firms. She was excited but hadn't been with her man for a couple weeks now and that was starting to really bother her, but she went and returned the following day. It was just what she needed as her business now flourished.

She informed them she could monitor their entire operation but had other customers to consider and wouldn't be able to accept a full blown contract. The executives had been so impressed with her accounting they were willing to allow her to monitor the subdivision she had just worked with and gave her a five year contract that increased her exposure and her income. Soon her income doubled right away as she picked up more business now from several local industry leaders. She hired several more people. And soon had her operation running very smoothly, having more time for herself like before and would soon spend time with Carl. She missed him so very much. When she saw him at work sometimes she would just go downstairs to his office just to get a hug, that helped some but didn't help too much because between her legs was a burning fire that only he could extinguish. Finally after the next several weeks had passed and a few weekends, after moving her office, she began feeling more comfortable and it was running just as she intended, she decided to spend a weekend with Carl and after going home that Friday, and had called home earlier and had Yan pack some clothes because they were both spending the weekend with him. She brought Yan along and when she arrived that Friday evening ran into Carl's arms and she held him for a very long time, he kissed her and could feel her heat, they were standing in the garage when he reached down and put his hand on her thigh, she was still in her work clothes as he rubbed the damp and very moist spot on her panty hose she wore as she quickly erupted and he just held her, she shook and buried her head in his chest and said in a weak voice she couldn't take it anymore, she had to be with him. She was as beautiful as ever in her business suit. Carl finally led her inside and upstairs, he had observed her at work and she was so sexy in her hi-heels and business suits. He turned and observed Betty kissing Yan as they talked and then they all headed upstairs.

When he got her to the bedroom he undressed her and she became like jelly in his arms, he felt her all over as she laid on the bed. He made love to her until she just couldn't move any longer after having several long organisms. Carl placed his face between her warm wet thighs and licked her vulva lips and caressed her clitoris as she lost all control as another massive organism racked her body. After that he licked her body and breast as he slowly climbed on top of her as he held her arms down against the bed. He then talked to her in a very loving way, as she was just lying there feeling totally exhausted. When she had regained some of her strength he led her, placing her in the large oversized pedestal bath tub letting her soak in some very warm water with bath oils. He then bathed her; it was the first time she had been in this tub as he kneeled down next to the tub and bathed her. She began crying a long time as tears ran down her face and said she loved him and told him she knew he loved her just by how he treated her. He had her stand as he rinsed her off and retrieved a large plush towel and wrapped her in it and dried her off before laying her down in the bed and lovingly massaging her with aromatic body oils. Before he finished she was sound asleep. He covered her and went downstairs where he found Betty and Yan in the kitchen and asked them to prepare a light meal and Yan suggested one he might like. He said that sounds very good as he hugged her and said welcome home, she smiled as he told them it would be about an hour before him and Sarah would be eating and they didn't have to wait on them if they were hungry. Carl returned upstairs and rubbed on a sleeping Sarah as he massaged her beautiful slim legs and played with her ass and her entire body. The more he rubbed on her tired body the harder she seemed to sleep, he rolled her over and rubbed her chest playing with her more and after half an hour she started to wake; she opened her eyes and saw him and felt his hands on her and smiled, Carl said welcome home baby girl.

Sarah reached out for him, telling her they were going downstairs to eat very soon and pulled her up and held her, said he missed her. He got her to dress in an oversized t-shirt and they went downstairs just as Yan finished cooking, Betty had set the table for two as Yan dished them up and Betty brought their food to the table. Sarah asked Betty to come here and gave her a big hug; Betty hugged her back and said welcome home mistress Sarah. Then Carl and Sarah sat down to eat and Carl really enjoyed Yans cooking. Carl looked at Sarah and knew it wouldn't be long before she would be asleep again, especially after a couple drinks. They ate, finished and Carl took Sarah outside on the deck and she just relaxed and stretched out and told him she needed that, meaning the sex and now was feeling so much better. Betty and Yan then ate and cleaned up the kitchen and Betty informed him that they had finished cleaning up. He checked and found everything in order. Yan asked Master Carl could Betty and her have one another. Carl said after he and Sarah had turned in for the night, and not before ten. Betty and Yan both said, thank you Master Carl. He returned to the deck with a couple bottles of water and Sarah eyes were closed as he touched her and told her to come with him, taking her upstairs and sitting on the bedroom couch as he fixed her a nice potent drink, she wasn't much conversation. She finished her drink and had her undress as he put her to bed and pulled the covers back and she fell asleep right away, he rubbed her some more and all she did was snore. Sarah was so tired he sat and drank alone. He found Betty and Yan and took them downstairs and fixed them a drink and sat and talked to both of them, and after they had finished their drinks told them to clean themselves and he might come up and watch them make love to one another. They said, thank you Master Carl as they went upstairs. Carl started closing the house up and soon went upstairs and undressed and climbed in bed with Sarah.

The next morning after waking up early, it being a Saturday as he put the coffee on and then returned upstairs, Sarah was still asleep and had slept a good ten to twelve hours. When she woke she ran to the bathroom and when she returned she climbed back in bed and he hugged her. Said she felt so much better now and she just couldn't sleep at home the way she slept here. Carl looked at her and said I wonder why. She kissed him and said it was because she felt safe here with him and Betty. She felt loved and Yan had told her she loved Betty and you treated her very well also. Sarah said she wanted to move in with him now; she couldn't take being away from him to much longer. Carl said to her whenever you're ready he and Betty were here for her and Yan. Carl said the coffee is ready; he left Sarah sitting on the bed and headed downstairs. Before going downstairs he went and knocked on Betty's door before entering, and found her and Yan in bed hugging one another, they rose after he entered and said time to get up, left and headed downstairs and poured his coffee and ate a donut. When he looked up Betty, Sarah and Yan were all hugging one another, it warmed his heart to see them embrace one another after that fateful holiday weekend. He sat in the morning sun on the deck drinking his coffee and was happy they were getting along, and was soon was joined by Sarah. Sarah told him she would start looking to move in but needed to recover from the office move first. Asked if she could bring some stuff over and Carl said let him think about it and would come up with a plan, she said ok, and drank her coffee. Yan came outside and said they could come inside and eat and that breakfast was ready. Betty had set the dining room table for two and Sarah and Carl ate and were served by both Betty and Yan.

They finished eating and enjoyed themselves the rest of the day swimming, showering and napping together and soon it was dinner time and Betty and Yan surprised them with a beautiful dinner and had set the dining room table with candles, they ate and when they finished he called Betty and Yan in and stood and thanked them and hugged each and told them he loved them very much, Yan began to cry and hugged him and said, thank you master Carl, he held her and said no, thank you very much Yan. Betty became so overcome with him hugging Yan she began to cry as he then hugged them both together. Sarah said thank you, and told them they made her feel very much loved. Carl helped the tearful pair clear the table as they washed the dishes. Then he and Sarah headed for the basement to have a much needed drink. After a while they shot some pool and had another drink. Betty came downstairs and said that they were finished and asked him if she and Yan could have each other again and he said yes, after they straightened his bedroom out and to clean the bath tub and the rest could wait until tomorrow. She said yes sir master, and departed. Sarah had heard Bettys request and said they deserve each other as her and Carl continued to play pool and then sat and had another drink. They called it an evening after a couple hours and showered, then massaged each other and went to bed, getting there rest as they held each other. Yan and Betty were in love with each other and they felt and performed oral sex on one another with both having multiple climaxes before falling asleep in each other's arms.

Carl woke up, and as usual went to the bathroom and freshened up before returning to bed and looking at Sarah, she was sleeping hard, he decided to get back up and fix some coffee, as he entered the hallway found he was right behind Betty and Yan on their way downstairs. He said good morning girls and they responded, good morning master. They fixed the coffee and poured him a cup when it finished brewing. He drank it and returned to see if Sarah was awoke, she was just starting to open her eyes when he returned, he asked her if she slept well to which she responded she had. He kissed her as she rose to freshen herself. He waited until she came out and hugged her and pulled her into the bed and kissed her as he felt her slim and shapely body. She loved him and returned his affections. He sat up and told her time to start a new day as she dressed and they went downstairs together and were served by their two servants. They soon ate and sat in the living room after he picked the Sunday paper up out of the driveway. Carl noticed there was a sale on at Four Girls and said it was time to get Betty and Yan some new clothing to wear around the house. Sarah said that sounded like a good idea. He asked her if she thought about what she would move here and what she wouldn't. Sarah said all of her art and accessories, and mostly all the furniture because he had the space for everything and her furniture would blend in very well with his, he agreed and then she asked him about where Yan would stay. He said she and Betty can share the same bedroom she was in already because it was large enough for the both of them; he would get a second chair for the room or another small couch. Sarah said she had both so that was taken care of.

He asked her what she wanted to do today and she said sleep, which was all she wanted, was to sleep and have him next to her. He told her that was fine with him and they spent a very relaxing day together. They ate later and continued to relax as Carl explored the newspaper and set the classifieds aside with a few circled sections. Later when it was late he and Sarah frolicked in the bed before taking a shower and going to sleep.

# Fourteen

The next couple of months went very smoothly for Sarah's company and it turned out to be financially beneficial as well, she picked up several more large corporate clients with some giving her long term contracts over several years, the number of people she employed had just about doubled and she had to create and made her longest and most trusted employee Carol Gene the head office manager and with two junior managers under her. She had ran the office in Sarah's absence before, only this time giving her one of the larger and empty and more private cubicle offices next to hers and added a generous pay raise to go with the added responsibilities, at double what she had paid her before. It worked out very well for Sarah and it allowed her to better oversee her company's complete and total operation. It wasn't long before she was asking Carl about the other half of the second floor, he said now, you will have to pay a little more than just ten dollars a month, it was an easily negotiated agreement since all he charged her was a thousand a month and having the entire second floor. She contacted the same contractors and in no time had the entire floor the way she desired. Her staff had increased again, close to thirty people now. Carl remodeled the break area downstairs by greatly expanding the space and adding a larger variety and more vending machines, and also more comfortable seating and moving the old picnic style tables, some to the warehouse break areas and to one that was located outside. Before Sarah's company moved in the building,

Carl's building maintenance department was able to keep the public areas clean and only had to do them once or twice a week or as needed and preformed a general cleanup. But after Sarah's company moved in there was so much more foot traffic it now required a full time custodian to maintain and clean the public spaces and all the washrooms and so he and Sarah decided on hiring a couple of people, a man and a woman to keep the washrooms, hallways and break areas clean in the entire building and split the cost, but they would be part of the building maintenance staff so they could perform any needed minor repairs as well.

Sarah had become so involved at work with the increased business, and increasing staff she still hadn't found the time to move in with Carl, but did start spending most of her weekends with him even though she slept most of the time. She and Yan both said when she spent the weekends and week nights at home she was very restless and didn't get any meaningful rest and it made her finally make up her mind to move in with him. She soon began contemplating her move and just took a week off and spent the time packing, hired a mover and just had everything moved to his home finally in one day. Carl had the other two bedrooms painted in the colors she had chosen over a month before and had a crew complete the job in a day as the house smelled like fresh paint for a day or two. After that had been accomplished Carl and her spent quite a few afternoons moving and arranging her furniture around, hanging pictures and just placing things in and around the very large home. Her complete bedroom set went into one of the empty bedrooms with several other pieces from around her home and her couch blended in with his in the living room and the house finally looked like someone really did live there. Betty and Yan ended up with a love seat in there room and a couple more chairs. After a month they were just about finished moving and arraigning everything the way they wanted.

Sarah began to slept so much better now and wasn't as tired when she went to work. Betty and Yan were extremely happy being with each other. Carl took them both with him to do the grocery shopping once a week and several times took them to the Four Girls and to several other stores to make personal purchases. He treated them very well and Betty purchased her and Yan some stocking, body suits, dresses and high heels so when Carl decided to take the group out to dinner they would look presentable. Sarah ended up being less uptight and treated both Betty and Yan much better now, but she was still very demanding at times and was still there mistress and they both respected that and loved her.

After Sarah had moved in, he and Sarah checked out her now very empty home as he made notes of the needed repairs and things he felt needed to be done to improve the property, it didn't amount to very much but he sent in a crew to paint the entire house, clean the carpets and make all the minor repairs that were needed. When Sarah decided to sell, Carl sold her home and it sold remarkable quickly through his real estate operation which ended up occupying the very last empty office space in his building after he had made it a completely separate business and eventually hired a permeant managing real estate broker to manage the new operation and moved his complex rentals to it along with the secretary who handled all the rental operations. Sarah received all the proceeds from the sale of her home minus the mortgage and didn't have to pay hardly anything but the sales commission and Carl's real estate office sold it above market value for more than the asking price. Sarah was elated and they soon went to the court house and acquired a marriage license.

It was a couple months later before they were actually married and had a very simple wedding, Betty and Yan were the bride's maids and John his best man. They held a small reception at their lovely home and it went very well. Yan and Betty served the guest. They went to a nearby resort and spa for their honeymoon, leaving Betty and Yan at home. Both had been away from running their businesses for over a week, when they returned they quickly began getting back into the swing of things. Carl hired her company and asked her to do an audit of his operations and she personally oversaw that one herself, and called him up to her office one day when it was finally complete. She handed him the report, he was due a large tax refund of several hundred thousand dollars and all his assets exceeded two hundred forty million dollars, it was mostly in real estate holdings, and his personal assets which were close to forty million. She said now that they were married she had to audit herself and her assets were her company and it was valued at, based on her profits around twenty million a year gross and her personal wealth only totaled close to sixteen million. She recommended leaving everything separate for tax purposes but they had placed one another on their banking accounts and other documents including assets and also had made out new wills and trust documents. She said she had undervalued the real estate based on true market values, deprecation and the cost of maintenance. He told her he was very satisfied as they stood and hugged and kissed. He told her he had to go because he had a contract he was going to bid on and would see her later at home. They told each other how much they loved one another as they kissed and hugged before he departed.

They were doing extremely well as individuals and as a couple. One Friday afternoon Sarah said it was time they had a little fun with Betty and Yan. It had been a while since they had tied or whipped either one and Betty had asked him several times to whip her and he just spanked her and played with her or stuck the phone activated dildo in her and watched her squirm as he had her handcuffed. He had them clean the house nude several times just as a reminder of who was in charge. Now that Sarah was settled and getting more relaxed and becoming less tired, he noticed she was getting back to thinking more about sex. One weekday he peered inside the extra bed room where her bedroom suit ended up and Sarah had Yan kneeling on the floor nude and Sarah's legs were wide open as she had Yan servicing her, it was exciting for him to watch as he watched her lick her mistress. After she had climax, Yan continued to lick her until Sarah told her to stop. Sarah lay back on the bed as Yan cleaned up in the bathroom. After Yan left he came into the room and lay next to her, and asked her if she felt better now, she said yes and asked him how he felt. Carl said it was time for a training session as he felt on Sarah and getting her even more aroused and talking dirty to her, then he abruptly stopped, stood and left as she called him to come back, and he said later, he had done it on purpose getting her hot and excited and she knew it. He liked getting her worked up and leaving her excited at times, then he would catch her later off guard and bring her to a rousing climax by surprise. One day she saw him make Betty suck him off and it made her so excited she played with herself and climaxed while watching them. They had told one another these things and they had a very active and most enjoyable sex life with one another and with both Yan and Betty. They even watched Betty and Yan together and made them do each other using dildos for their entertainment sometimes which Betty and Yan both enjoyed doing.

One Friday evening, they especially liked Fridays because it marked the beginning of their weekend because he and Sarah didn't work weekends unless there was a problem at their operations or an emergency. Yan and Betty were always prepared for something to happen on Friday especially after dinner. He and Sarah went to sit on the deck together, Carl asked Sarah what should we have the girls to do to entertain us, Sarah thought about it a long while before she said, maybe we should have them dress up in the body suits they purchased, she said those are so sexy with the hi-heels on and then we will decide. He called the girls and told them what to wear and told them he wanted them to also wear some makeup and lipstick. Very soon about half an hour later, after he and

Sarah had decided to go downstairs to the basement both women appeared before them. Carl poised them and took many pictures and then cuffed them and continued photographing them and said they were really beautiful. Then he inserted the phone activated dildos and hung them from the ceiling and took even more pictures, he told Sarah they looked so very lovely and he was getting so aroused just looking at them. They turned on their phones and brought the app up and watched both girls dance around having multiple organisms as they sat and had their drinks, and when they thought they had enough turned them off. Carl let them hang there a long while before unhooking them and removed the cuffs as both women found it very difficult to stand up. Carl fixed them some potent drinks after having them remove and cleanup the dildos. Then had them sit at the bar and drink what he had fixed for them. Sarah made Betty stand next to her as she felt her and told Carl she wanted her, they finished their drinks before taking Betty and Yan upstairs to the spare bedroom which turned out to be a playroom more now since Sarah had moved in. They all undressed and Sarah took Betty and he took Yan and they just had their way with their willing servants and had their own private orgy.

Carl felt all over Yan as she became so very excited and fingered her as she climaxed very easily after the episode in the basement and he climbed on top of her for the first time and slid into her tight but wet vagina and soon she was climaxing as he fingered her tight little ass, she said oh master Carl as he turned her over and entered her from the rear and played with her ass some more as it became more relaxed and after having several fingers inside of her soon slid his penis inside of her anus and very soon she was comfortable with it inside of her playing with her clit as she climaxed again. Betty and Sarah were on top of each other with each eating the other out as Sarah came first then Betty, and soon they were kissing and fingering one another. The room smelled of sex as Carl took Yan to the showers and rammed his man hood in her ass again after he had lathered it up with soap and inserting several fingers inside her vagina and playing with her clit as she continued climaxing again. He then gave her a golden shower before he bathed himself and then her. They were drying off as Sarah and Betty entered and continued their wild lust filled exploits and bathing one another.

Carl and Yan applied massage oils to one another as Yan said she loved her master Carl and they kissed and held each other as Betty and Sarah emerged and did the same with the oils, Betty and Sarah continued to kiss as they applied oil before they laid back exhausted still holding one another. Betty curled up in Sarah's arms as she held her tight. Carl suggested he should order them a couple of pizzas and they all agreed that would be fine. He departed and placing the order as he pulled some money from his wallet and put on some clean shorts and a t-shirt. When he returned found Sarah holding both Yan and Betty. They were all smiling and happy. Carl sat on the side of the bed and Yan came and hugged him. He stood pulling Sarah up and hugged her and they kissed saying she was so very happy now. He told Betty and Yan to put on some t-shirts and panties for when the pizza came. Carl went downstairs found a plastic table cloth and spread it out along with some paper plates and some paper towels. Went to the basement and returned with a chilled bottle of red wine and some glasses, and waited for the delivery which came soon since it had been almost an hour since he called. When the doorbell rang he paid for the pizzas as his group came downstairs looking very sexy and hungry. They all dug in and this time there wasn't anything left over. They drank the wine until the bottle was empty. Carl said for them all to sit up at least an hour and not to lie down. Betty and Yan cleaned up and then he said everyone to the basement as he served them more wine. Sarah and Betty sat and talked and were soon hugging and then dancing, since Carl had turned the radio on as he shot some pool. Yan asked if she could play. Yan wasn't bad at the game and even won one of the three games before he decided it was time for them to all go to bed. They all went upstairs. He secured the house and soon followed. He brushed his teeth and climbed into bed with Sarah and they held and felt on each other before falling asleep.

Saturday he awoke and Sarah was coming out the bathroom and got right back in bed, he kissed her and also went into the bathroom himself, and soon returned to the bedroom. She told him she had never had another woman before like what had transpired between her and Betty and was happy she had the opportunity. Said she knew Betty was clean and was one reason she just let herself go, and thanked him for not being jealous and allowing her the freedom to be herself, she asked him did he enjoy Yan, and he said yes, very much and was happy she was as open minded as she was to allow him to have another woman and to be their when it happened. Sarah said she loved Betty and Yan and was happy they were a part of their household. Told Carl she wouldn't be jealous of them or him together, he said the same went for her and them. She said thank you master Carl as they then hugged one another and kissed and just laid there in bed. There was a knock at the door and Betty came in with Yan and said they wanted to be with Carl and her and said they loved them and Sarah pulled Betty to her as she curled up and Sarah held her, Betty said she wanted Sarah again as she cried and Sarah held her, Yan climbed in with Carl and he held her and felt her and soon caused her to have a climax. Betty slid down between Sarah thighs and she opened them wide as Betty buried her head in Sarah crotch and soon she had a massive climax as she held Carl's hand and they kissed. They all laid together a little more than an hour kissing on one another.

Carl said its time to get up and have something to eat, he kissed Yan and she went to her room to wash up as Betty soon followed as he and Sarah cleaned up and then went downstairs together. Everyone ate and Carl suggested they take Betty and Yan with them to dinner later, she said that sounds great. When they finished eating Carl checked things around the house and walked around outside before returning after having checked the pool water and adding some chemicals and placing the droid cleaner in the pool. When he returned Yan was running the vacuum and Betty was changing the sheets and making up the beds then they proceeded to clean all the bathrooms. Yan and Betty had worked out who would do what between themselves and Carl and Sarah had the cleanest house since it was cleaned everday. He found Sarah looking through her clothes, trying to decide what to wear later, the weather was very pleasant, comfortable and warmer than usual. She decided to wear a close fitting one piece black dress with an open back and thin shoulder straps; with open toe low heel dress shoes and a matching purse. Then she would pick what Yan and Betty would wear, she knew Carl had taken them both shopping several times just for such occasions like this. Sarah in her mind had stopped looking at Betty so much as a slave or servant and the same applied to Yan and more like their wards. For Carl they were his concubines and he loved her for being so opened minded and couldn't ask for more.

Sarah looked in Betty's closet and asked her after she had finished cleaning the bathrooms to show her what Carl had her buy for herself; she had several very nice dresses. Betty told Sarah she had her own account and had paid for the dresses and that master Carl just made suggestions and had her try them on before she bought them showing her the shoes with matching purses and told her that she had to dress and look like she belonged to someone. Sarah agreed and said she would let her decide on her own what to wear. Betty thanked her and kissed Sarah and asked Betty to show her what Carl bought for Yan. Betty and Yan shared the same large closet and Carl had bought Yan some cute and sexy dresses, shoes and purses also and Sarah said she was satisfied and left their bedroom and returned to hers. Carl had just finished making reservations for them at the

Italian Gardens and looking to see what he would wear, and pretty much knew, one of his summer suits and a dress t-shirt with sandals.

It was midafternoon when he after dressing went to see what Betty and Yan were wearing. Betty wore a dress that was above the knee, was pale blue with a low cut collar in front and back, was sleeveless, she wore open toed shoes without stockings and a matching purse and shoes that matched the dress, her hair was in a bun and she worn earrings and had polished her short but cute nails with clear polish and the same for her toes, Carl complimented her on her very sex appearance. Yan wore a short above the knee green one piece sleeveless dress, earrings and a small gold chain, her hair was in a large thick braid and she carried a small green purse with matching green open toe hi heels with green nail polish on her toes and hands. Sarah wore the black one piece dress, with black open toe hi heels, a pearl necklace and earrings, with pink finger nails and toes. When Carl had them all in the living room he took several pictures with Sarah in the middle and then individually as they prepared to depart. They were all very beautiful and happy.

Riding in Sarah's car, Carl drove, and they soon arrived at the restaurant, Carl used the valet parking as they all walked inside and approached the maître and his beautiful group was promptly seated in a large comfortable booth. They were such a lovely group. The waiter soon approached and Carl ordered a bottle of wine for them as they looked over the menu deciding on what they wanted. Carl proposed a toast to the family. He and

Sarah sat next to one another and she complimented Betty and Yan on their beautiful and sexy appearance and said she was very proud of them. The waiter returned and they all ordered. Carl held Sarah's hand and kissed it. He looked at each woman and was proud of each one. Soon their food arrived. Sarah said she was proud of them because they had such poise and were very graceful and beautiful. After finishing their meal and he was the only one who had desert, they soon departed, and Carl suggested they go to the mall and walk around. They arrived and walked around and window shopped, Carl just wanted to look at them since they were so sexy and cute, especially since they were all dressed up. He sat on a bench and just watched them for a while before deciding they were ready to go heading directly home. When they got home he took more pictures of them. Everyone left to put on some shorts and t-shirts. They had walked there food down and Carl asked them to come downstairs to the bar and fixed them some nice drinks to loosen them up. He had really enjoyed last night and told Sarah how he felt and said she felt the same way. Soon Betty was feeling like she wanted to be used and told them so; he then began feeling between her legs and got her very aroused and then stopped, making her suffer by not letting her climax. He brought back a hand vibrator and a pair of handcuffs as he cuffed her arms behind her back and ran the vibrator all over her body and removed her shirt and played with her nipples and soon she exploded with a massive climax.

Sarah soon grabbed Yan between her legs as she licked her face and ear and soon she climaxed, then noticed Carl was hard and she knelt down and pulled his shorts down and placed him in her mouth and began sucking him, then Betty joined her and finally Yan, he came as they all licked him clean. He stood, un-cuffed Betty and had to fix another drink after that, he had never had that happen in his life. The women after that kissed each other as he looked on. They laughed and drank some more and then he said they should all go upstairs and he helped them and Sarah wanted them all to sleep together as they undressed and climbed into Carl's large bed having a wonderful time with each other. Yan sat on top of him as Sarah kissed him and Betty kissed Yan and soon everyone had climaxed as they rolled off one another and soon they all fell into a deep sleep together. Sarah had a smile on her face and sleep like a baby. Carl held her and Betty held him as Yan held Betty. When they woke the next morning they all showered together and he took Betty again. Afterwards they all oiled up then they all rubbed on Carl together which was so very exciting. He said he couldn't take any more and they decided it was time to eat. They were all still tired and a little hung over as they ate breakfast and when they finished, felt so much better. Carl said it had been the most exciting weekend he had ever experienced and thanked them for such a wonderful time, told them not to touch him today, he had to regain his strength. He opened the upstairs windows as Yan stripped down the beds and made them up; and Betty cleaned the bathrooms they had used.

Carl had decided and planned to cook dinner. He liked to cook and took some chicken out to thaw and would season it later and headed to the basement. Sarah came downstairs as he held her and kissed her as she now became real excited especially after he cuffed her and hung her from the ceiling and ripped the t-shirt open she had on, feeling her all over playing with her as she trembled and he knelt and licked and sucked her clit holding her legs wide open as she had several uncontrollable orgasms because once she started climaxing he didn't stop licking and sucking her vagina. When he stood up again in front of her she had a smile on her face and when he released her she collapsed into his arms, weak and very exhausted. Told her he wanted to make love to his wife and told her she could rest now taking her up on the elevator and placed her in the freshly made up bed. She went right to sleep again then he went back downstairs to the kitchen and started seasoning the chicken and placing it in the refrigerator before returning upstairs and lying down beside Sarah. Sarah slept as he rubbed on her. He took a quick nap and when she woke found him next to her and rubbed on him until he woke up and climbed on top of him and just laid there kissing him. He looked at the clock and said he would cook today. She said great, they got up, dressed and headed downstairs. Betty and Yan were napping in there room when Sarah went to see where they were and decided not to wake them.

Carl liked cooking and prepared all he was going to cook; lightly steamed mixed vegetables, seasoned rice and a salad and soon had it all ready and began cooking. Sarah sat and they talked as she watched and he soon finished, and all was ready as she set the table. She left to tell Yan and Betty to come eat. When they came downstairs he dished up there plates and he served them with a chilled red wine and just asked them to have a seat. He blessed the table and said eat up ladies, they ate and feed their famished bodies, and they thanked him for such a wonderful and tasty meal. Betty cried and said she never felt so loved for once in her miserable life and found it hard to composed herself and said thank you master Carl and Mistress Sarah for having her in their life. Yan thanked them also and Carl said enough just eat and be thankful we have each other now. They ate and they all kissed him afterwards as Yan and Betty began cleaning up as he put away the small amount of rice that was left over. When Betty and Yan finished he had them out on the deck drinking a wine punch he made and told them to relax. Sarah said you are a kind and wonderful person, that's one of the reasons she loved him so much. After an hour the temperature had risen since a very warm breeze from the south sweep across the area and it became extremely warm outside almost ninety degrees as the humidity also rose. Carl told them all to undress and get in the pool and swim in the nude, they did including him and after an hour he got out went inside and returned with some large bath towels. They stayed in the pool since it was refreshing being outdoors and in the water. Soon after they started getting out and he handed each a towel. It was getting late as he and Sarah needed their rest and told Betty and Yan they needed to shower and oil themselves before going to bed, they kissed him and Sarah and went inside as he and Sarah closed and locked up the house, turning on the climate control system since tomorrow was supposed to be even warmer and much more humid. He closed and locked all the windows downstairs and then upstairs before he went and took a shower washing the pool water off, then he and Sarah oiled themselves before getting in bed together as they hugged and kissed before soon falling asleep.

# Fifteen

The following weeks and months continued to be really beneficial for both Carl's and Sarah's business ventures, she secured several more major clients, and didn't need any additional staff, but had to make and subdivide her operation more, giving her office manager two more assistant managers. She needed to do that in order to maintain the high standards she already had achieved and to also maintain better control. Pay raises also went with the positions and were coveted by all the employees who held them.

Carl on the other hand had bought out another small electrical supplier and the building they were located in and operated it as a satellite operation for a short while until he absorbed and merged their entire inventory into his before he closed the location and was going to sell the building to some people who wanted to make a restaurant out of it. The buyout allowed him to operate under another very trusted name in the industry and gave him even more clients and extended his customer base making him one of the largest wholesale electrical and plumbing suppliers now in a three state region, and also allowing him to drastically cut his wholesale prices and increase his market share even more. When the deal to sell the property fell through; he ended up selling it to the village it was located in; since they needed a newer building for one of their maintenance departments. He also bought several older apartment buildings that were well built brick buildings with style, but had fallen into disrepair over the years, and he did complete gut rehabs and then added them to his inventory of investment properties, buying them below market prices and bringing them up to date and operated some of them as luxury rentals but most he sold as condos through his thriving real estate operation. His heating and air-conditioning business was picking up and had added three new crews since he married Sarah. He completely replaced his fleet of trucks with some of the newest high cube vans to keep his fleet up to date and to also lower his vehicle maintenance cost since the truck dealers were overstocked with inventory making the purchases less expensive. He had picked up some additional maintenance contracts for several large big box stores and a few more industrial locations. His business was steady and growing. His income also increased and it was constant and he never had any idle crews.

Carl finally decided on purchasing a new vehicle, and bought one with all the bells and whistles. He kept his old car since Betty knew how to drive and ended up letting her use it so her and Yan could grocery shop and run errands and then he didn't have to bother taking them grocery shopping, though he did go with them every now and then. That worked out very well for them all as Betty seemed to get out of the funk she had been in due to Harold's treatment of her over the many years of abuse and Yan seemed even much happier now also, since he wanted them to be as happy as possible, and really loved them both. He never mentioned to Sarah about Harold's plan to murder Betty even though he really wanted to but felt it would be too much for her to handle and just left it alone since it was in the past and Betty didn't have a very clear memory of what had actually happened anyway and since she seemed to have found a new life living with him and Sarah and Yan companionship help her transformation and she seemed so much happier now. Carl referred to the old saying of letting sleeping dogs lie, so they say. He and Sarah took each other to lunch just about every day and soon he appointed John to be the new general manager, a position he created to oversee really everything in his place including the heating and air conditioning, electrical and plumbing portion of his operation after remodeling his offices again a second time. He reorganized all his operations and offices, and divided them into separate divisions. He had already separated the real estate operations before this new re-origination. The air-conditioning, plumbing and electrical service was a separate company and organized to handle the calls for all service work. That was handled by a secretary who scheduled the job request as they came in and the others were routine and or regularly scheduled maintenance. That worked out so much better even if two crews showed up for the same job, just as before with each handling a particular portion of the job, it made for quicker response times and more satisfied customers. The roofing and rehab were separated and both generated a handsome profit on their own. He had a lot of repeat customers which helped his better business rating and consumer ratings stay highly rated. Soon he was ranked number one in the area bringing in even more business. He spent less time in the office now and more time checking out other business opportunities. He even purchased a mall that had closed, it was in a depressed commercial area, was very outdated and really beyond repair. He had it demolished and cleared the vast property which was about one hundred and sixty acres. The taxes were much cheaper on vacant land as he explored what would be profitable to build there. He looked at a possible amusement park, hotel, apartment complex, and even condos. There were new residential developments in the surrounding area as he watched closely the area sales for a long while, but the land was a good tax write off and he would just sit on it until it proved feasible to redevelop it, and Sarah's business kept close tabs on his operations and preformed semiannual audits.

One weekday afternoon Carl decided to leave work early and went home after stopping and picking up some beer and other spirits. After he entered the house and put the beer away he was greeted by Yan who was vacuuming. He went to his bed room to change clothes and shortly there was a knock at the door and there stood Betty. He said come in and she approached him and knelt down before him with her arms out stretched with a whip in her hands, she looked up at him and said please master Carl, please whip me, he looked at her and just decided to give her what she wanted as he told her to stand. He looked at her and asked her why she wanted him to whip her now. She said it felt good to her and had missed it so much and said it had been a long time since she was whipped, said she knew she was much loved here but needed and wanted it badly. He asked her if she wanted him to hang her in the basement, and she said, yes please, Master Carl. He asked if she had finished her duties around the house, yes she replied, and said Yan was now finishing up. He told her as he continued to change into some shorts and t-shirt to go wait for him downstairs. He finished changing and soon headed downstairs. There she stood, where she had always stood before a punishment since being here. She had already undressed and she was looking so much better than the first time when he met her now almost three years earlier. The last time he checked her she had gained twenty-nine pounds, her breast were now full and firm, she appeared better than ever before and her skin was smooth, soft, and tight, she looked good and so very sexy. He looked into her eyes; kissed her and told her, you know Betty my dear, this really isn't necessary. She begged him and said please whip me master, make me happy master, please master Carl, please. He went to the cabinet and removed the cuffs and returned cuffing her wrist together and attached them to a chain above her head. Her breast were so much fuller now as were her hips and thighs as he felt and caressed her body in a manner that soon aroused her very much and the way he purposely touched her to make her even more sensitive as he now went to the cabinet where all the restraint equipment was now kept. He soon returned with the thin leather whip he preferred using. It stung when it made contact with flesh, she had told him so. He told her to spread her legs after bringing back the ankle cuffs and the spreader bar, attaching them to her ankles as she looked down at him in anticipation of what was to follow. He finished attaching the ankle cuffs and bar and he was looking directly at her vagina, he kissed it and pulled the hood back that covered her very large clitoris and placed it between his lips, she shivered as he licked and sucked the sensitive bud before he stood and looked into her face as she pleaded for him to please whip her. He felt her again between her legs while kissing her, she responded to his sensitive touch and almost climaxed. Then he stepped back, raising the strap up and struck her vagina several times very hard, then her butt and thighs, her back and stomach repeatedly without stopping and across her breast several times all over her until tears ran down her pretty face, and her skin started to show the thin red whelps from the whipping, he stopped and held her head with one hand and slapped her. Looking at her and then asking her, what do you say now? Betty said thank you master Carl. He felt her between her legs and touched her swollen vagina and soon brought her to a rousing climax whispering dirty disgusting things in her ear, causing her to climax several more times. Carl let her hang there until he could decide if she needed more or if he was finished with her. He looked into her pretty face and unhooked her, removed the cuffs and made her crawl to the elevator and took her upstairs to the spare bedroom where he had her kneel in bed where he slapped her ass hard several times before he threw her on her back and climbed on top of her and had rough sex with her, then made her kneel as he entered her again. She climaxed repeatedly before he entered her anus and he smacked her ass cheeks and filling her ass with hot sperm and pulling her around by the hair and having her lick him clean. Then he took her by the hair to the bathroom and had her kneel in the shower as he urinated in her mouth and all over her body, he pulled her up by her hair and slapped her again and told her how much of a slut she was then turned on the water and bathed her. He held her arms behind her as he entered her anus again after lathering her up as she now cried. When he finished and pulled her up to face him asked her if she was satisfied now. She shook her head and said yes sir, Master Carl. She began crying and hugged him tightly and said thank you master. They showered and bathed one another then dried off. He spread out a towel as he oiled her body and looked at the marks he had placed on her, when he finished she oiled him. When she finished she thanked him again as he sent her to put on some clean clothes.

Carl fixed a sandwich and had a beer, and thought about what had just happened. It had been several months since anything close to what he just did had happened, almost a year. Betty evidently was missing something she had grown accustomed to and needed some satisfaction from, at least the span of time before her episodes of need had increased by months and remembered when they only spanned a few weeks. Betty came into the kitchen and he made her sit next to him. He asked her why now after all this time did you want me to whip you. She told him she needed a reminder of what had brought her to this wonderful place, she wanted to feel the pain as a reminder of how well off she really was now and some unknown need she had from her past, she again said, thank you master Carl. She kissed him and cried as he held her as she continued crying a very long time. She recovered some and he told her to go lay down and he would see her later. He sent her to her room. Carl finished his sandwich and checked the outside of the house. Checked the pool and returned and took his vitamins.

Carl went himself and lay down and took a nap, he had been looking to expand his business by diversification but the economy was slowing down and he didn't want to be overextended in to many areas and decided to just let things run smoothly on their own for now. There was an abundance of properties on the market and no buyers and the number of foreclosures was gradually increasing, but the asking prices were too high to be of any benefit to him and only looked now for profitable rehab projects. He found a couple of older office building that were in suburban central business districts where restaurants were opening and some of these neighborhoods were undergoing gentrification and it kept his crews busy with the buildings being reconfigured. He added them to his real estate holdings and they proved to be very profitable over a short period of time as they helped his real estate holding and generated monthly profits. Carl fell asleep and didn't wake until Sarah came home. She had undressed and washed up before climbing in bed with him, kissing him as he hugged her. She asked him about his day and he told her about Betty. Sarah was a little surprised as he told her all he had done to her and what Betty had said. Sarah said well it's been quite a while and understood and said he hadn't tied her up in a while either. He said please not today. She laughed and kissed him as they lay together and she told him she loved him very much.

They both fell asleep and then woke up about an hour later and found Yan and Betty preparing dinner. Betty and Yan served them and it was a beautiful meal as usual. After Betty and Yan had finished eating they went outside and sat on the deck and talked about how the economy was slowing down and what their plans were going to be. He told her he wasn't going to expand anymore for a while until he saw a change in the markets and she also agreed with him that would be a smart move. They decided to go to the basement and have a drink. Sarah asked Carl if she should talk to Betty, he asked her why, what do you want to say to her, do you feel sorry for her, do you want to whip her, what are you feeling right now. Sarah actually didn't know, she loved Betty and told Carl so. Do you want to take her and maybe spank or whip her? He said let's do it together then, he said then he would feel better even if he just watched. Told her maybe you need to be punished also. He had never punished Sarah in front of Yan or Betty and asked her if her submission before them would make her happy. She said the thought very much excited her and she was getting wet thinking about it. He said it isn't Friday and Betty and Yan have come to expect something happening on Fridays and this would be a shock and surprise. He said yes maybe I should have all my bitches hanging and serving me, and as he said that it excited and made Sarah so hot she started feeling herself and Carl saw her and told her to stop, she didn't want to stop, and told him she could do what she wanted as she bated him, he told her to stop because she was his bitch, she refused as he came around and grabbed and held her

247

arms as she surrendered to him and said she was a dirty slut and could do what she wanted, whenever she wanted. He decided he would punish them all together as he told her to strip now bitch, she did without hesitation.

After telling Sarah to stand and strip, he brought the cuffs over and Carl placed them on her wrist and then raised her arms above her head and hooked them to the chains. He then went and chose a large butt plug and applied some lubricant to it and worked it up into her anus, she was now getting even more excited and as she did, he kissed her and sticking his tongue in her mouth as her nipples stood at attention in anticipation. Sarah was dripping wet with excitement as her anticipation was quickly rising, then he called for Betty and Yan to come downstairs. They soon appeared, Betty and Yan were both surprised and frightened and it showed on their faces as Carl told them both to undress, in a loud and commanding voice as he began belittling them. Betty undressed and Carl cuffed her hands together, hanging her also on one side of Sarah, then Yan as he cuffed her the same way and added another length of chain to an empty hook and hung her also on the other side of Sarah. Sarah was now in the middle and saw the marks on Betty's body which excited her. Carl went and got a butt plug and inserted one inside of Betty, then another one inside of Yan after lubing each one of their asses up before sitting at the bar and looking at them hanging there. He said they were all his bitches and could do whatever he wanted to them whenever he wanted because they were sluts, tramps and whores, his whores and were here to serve him as he saw fit, and now saw fit to punish there tramp asses all together. He decided to clamp their nipples and used the extra-large clothes pins as he applied them to each. Betty kept looking at Sarah and started to speak and Carl looked at her and told her to shut up bitch, you better not speak, she had never seen or imagined her being punished and began crying, because she loved her. Carl walked over to Betty and asked her why was she crying, said she loved Sarah and begged him not to hurt her. He looked at Betty and asked why she felt that way, said she cared about her and said please master whip me instead. He stepped back, took a whip and said he was the master and had decided to punish them all because as master he could, just for his own enjoyment. Yan appeared truly terrified and now urinated as Sarah pressed her knees together to keep from climaxing; Betty was now becoming really scared as Carl enjoyed the truly very terrified look on all their pretty faces. Yan now began to cry as he approached and placed a finger in her mouth and told her to suck it bitch. She did like never before and said she was going to lick her piss up off the floor when he finished with her sorry ass. Then took two pieces of rope and attached Bettys ankle to Sarah's and then Yan's to Sarah other ankle as all three were fairly stretched wide open between there thighs as he returned to the cabinet. All three began to tremble and shake now in pure terror and excitement as he told them they were his cunts and how he was going to expose them in public if they didn't obey and decided to blindfold them starting with Yan, then Betty and Sarah last as he finished. Carl went and sat at the bar and had a drink as he watch each woman as they stood spread open for his enjoyment and not knowing what would happen. Carl took out the handheld vibrator and first went and placed it on Yan vagina first as he played with her and applied the vibrator to her clit and she soon climaxed. He continued as she screamed and climaxed again and twisted the clothes pins, then he did Betty who climaxed very quickly as her pussy was still swollen and very sensitive from earlier as he twisted the clothes pins on her nipples, and finally Sarah who the anticipation had built up as soon as he touched her climaxed and then he continued applying the vibrator to her as multiple climatic spasms rocked her and she screamed and he twisted the clothes pins on her now swollen nipples. He went and fixed another drink and took pictures of all of them hanging. He asked them who am I, they all answered he was Master Carl. He removed the clothe pins from Yan and Betty and pinched there nipples as they screamed before he removed them from Sarah. He got the flogger whip, and whipped them all, their stomachs, thighs, calf, butts, and backs as they moaned. Suddenly he took the leather paddle with the long handle and smacked there pussies several times very hard as they each jerked violently doing each at least four to five times. Then he played with them until each climaxed and fingered them making them lick his fingers afterwards. He removed the blindfolds and kissed each one. Then he released their ankles leaving each one hanging before he released them and making them kneel in a tight circle before dropping his shorts and had them all suck him off together and they did, then afterwards he urinated on all three as they held their heads back with their mouths open and when he finished told them they were his bitches. He had them remove the cuffs from one another as he put his shorts back on. He had all three clean up after he removed the butt plugs. Then he said they were to the shower and afterwards line up and go upstairs to the second bed room and told them they could have each other as he watched.

Carl enjoyed watching their beautiful bodies intertwined as they satisfied there growing lust for one another and especially Sarah. Betty and Sarah were into each other and he took Yan and bent her over and enjoyed himself with her then as Sarah ate Betty, he entered her and she soon climaxed as Betty licked him and then her. It wasn't long before they all were exhausted, but very satisfied. They all went to shower and felt and kissed and cleaned each other before lying on the bed and oiling one another, Carl loved feeling on them and they liked it also. Sarah kissed him and said how exciting that had made her and how much better she felt now. Sarah said she wanted to sleep with Betty and would stay in this bed room with her tonight. He looked at Sarah and told her anything for you baby, and Yan slept with him. He took Yan with him and he fixed himself a drink and one for Yan and soon they were in bed together, he felt on her and soon she was very aroused again and having sex, he had her suck him as he ate her, she came before he did and he played with her until he did, then they held each other and fell asleep. Betty and Sarah had each other once again and feel asleep in each other's arms.

The following morning Carl called in and said he wouldn't be in, but call if they needed him for any reason, but knew John had things under control as well as his other managers. He and Yan showered together and enjoyed bathing together, said she loved him as she sat in his lap hugging him with him inside of her as she wrapped her legs around him and climaxed several more times. They showered again and oiled up as he put on some shorts and a t-shirt. She then went to her room to get something to wear. He and Yan went downstairs as he made the coffee as Yan began preparing breakfast. Soon Sarah and Betty came downstairs looking exhausted but very happy and Betty helped Yan with the food. Carl told Sarah he had called in and would be home today. Sarah checked her schedule and would skip today also and called and let her head office manager know. Sarah was in no condition to go in anyway. They all ate and were happy. It was good Betty and Yan had shopped a couple days before and they weren't in need of any food items. After breakfast Carl and Sarah went for a walk around the neighborhood. When they returned Carl and her laid down and discussed what had happened yesterday. Sarah said she was satisfied and very happy with him, loved him as she kissed him and he held her and they fell asleep.

When they woke it was early afternoon, they ate a light meal, sat up a little while. Everyone was in need of rest and after a while all of them went back to bed again.

# Sixteen

Carl and Sarah were very happy, and so were Betty and Yan. They ran their home with love and everyone was very happy. Sarah was very happy as she was able to be herself and free with her thoughts of a loving her husband and her fantasies of bondage and lesbianism and knowing he loved her very much. She was free of feeling jealousy and envy and knew she had found the perfect man for her. She went to work happy and came home happy.

Carl was happy with his wife and knew she loved him and was free to love her, and also Betty and Yan. Not many men would have a wife like Sarah, that was freaky and both open minded and he always had a smile on his face.

Betty had finally found what was missing in her life, what she had become after the tragic death of her child and all the years of abuse from Harold, she had found a place where she was loved and when she needed her special need filled, Carl and Sarah were there for her and had found that she wasn't all alone with a friend, lover, and companion in Yan.

Yan had found after an early life of abuse by being sold by her family into a life of servitude, a home where she was loved and had found a special friend and lover who shared a tormented past and now felt the comradery of not being alone anymore.

A household of very special people placed together by fate, the reasons would be obvious if one knew all the facts. But life has a strange way of protecting those who need divine help, even if the journey is at times convoluted.

# Finis